Pee On Water

Publishing Genius
www.publishinggenius.com

ISBN 10: 0-9820813-8-3
ISBN 13: 978-09820813-8-9

Stories in this collection previously appeared in the following
journals: *Puerto Del Sol*: "The Jon Lennin Xperience" *New York
Tyrant*: "The Magic Umbrella" and "Pee on Water" *Cincinnati
Review*: "McGrady's Sweetheart" *Unsaid*: "The Totems Are
Grand" *Barrelhouse*: "Doodle Face" *No Colony*: "My Boyfriend,
but Tragic" *Noo Journal*: "Dream House" *American Short Fiction*:
"Iconographic Conventions" *Elimae*: "The Kid" [*SIC*] *Journal*:
"The Sad Girlfriend"

Pee On Water

Rachel B. Glaser

Publishing Genius Press
Baltimore, Maryland

Stories

for Max & Mojo

The Magic Umbrella

One day there was a girl whose name was Jen. She was a secondgrader. Jen was running to catch the bus when she saw that it was raining. She ran back to get her umbrella. On the way she saw an umbrella walking towards her and it had a face! Jen was scared but she opened it anyway. It was taking her higher and higher, it took her to Mars. Millions of aliens walked in a big circle around her. They said "beep beep."

All the way back at school, the bus had arrived and the kids were playing outside. Rachel, Jen's best friend, was saying, "What is that noise?" It was the bell. All of the kids ran to their classrooms. They went in. The teacher said "Where is Jen?" No one knew. Right then Jen's voice said "Here I am." She had flown right through the window and into her chair!

All about the author. Agnes wrote this when she was seven. She grew up in Point Judith, a small shore town. The youngest of many siblings, she was still thoroughly bored by her family. Though known in Point Judith for her watercolor seascapes, Agnes found these unremarkable. Sloppy clouds dripped into the ocean. A bird's eyes smudged and looked like glasses. Her paper got waterlogged and wavy and her brushes frequently lost their hair. Occasionally, she attempted something really modern, but she knew her place. She was a young regional artist.

One time on a family retreat, they slept in tents by the sea. Morning light seeped through the tent in a friendly, inclusive way and she was last to wake. The sea made its wushing sound, like it was washing itself. Breakfast was cooked over a fire. Agnes looked dreamily into the fire. The others had run off to play. It was just her and her uncle. She felt grown up on her own, without the crowd of her family. The fire reached up into the air and then was stopped by air. She looked closely at the embers, where she saw the shape of a face. Her uncle said he had a weird dream the night before. The telling of the dream went on and on. She did not care for the dream.

Eventually, her uncle left her staring at the fire. The face in the fire was not just a coincidence of shapes. The fire was a creature and picked itself off the ground. The fire thing looked at Agnes. "I hate when people retell their dreams," he said. Agnes could barely hear his voice, it was so crackly. His legs were made of sticks—his arms, head, feet, knees, all sticks on fire. He walked with a snapping sound. Agnes followed the fire man to the ocean, where he extinguished his flames. Then he was just sticks and wood. "I have two styles," the stick man said, "on fire, or just sticks." Then he swam a bit in the ocean while Agnes watched. He was an excellent swimmer. Water shot through his arms. A couple sticks broke off and bobbed in the sea.

Agnes's brother walked up and said "What's new, Stupid?" Agnes ignored him and he left laughing. She could see her stick man in the distance and she watched him fight the tide toward her.

All eyes turned when they stepped into the saloon. A man said "Leave that firewood outside!" Agnes was about to explain when everyone in the saloon cracked up because they were all friends with the stick man. The bartender stopped to shake his hand. There were lanterns and whale nets hanging from the walls. People were dancing to a banjo player in the back. A drink was placed in front of Agnes, but she was afraid.

The man of sticks drank his drink and another was placed before him. A beautiful woman walked by and lit his head on fire with a match, flirting. His head had flames like hair. Then the woman blew smoke from the stick man into another man's eyes. The stick man didn't have the kind of mouth that smiled, but Agnes knew he was happy. He asked the beautiful woman to dance and left Agnes alone with her drink.

The stick man and beautiful woman danced song after song, while Agnes wondered where her family was. Her drink sat in front of her, taunting her. It was the kind you were supposed to drink quick like medicine. The bartender looked at her suspiciously. Though she looked very human, she was the one who stuck out at the saloon, not the man of sticks! Her whole summer had been like this. At the fair, she'd win the raffle, and then the prize would be something worse than nothing. She'd follow a recipe exactly and still the food would taste like laundry. All these people had already met her magic stick man. She closed her eyes and drank the drink. It tasted like poison and then it warmed her chest.

With a vague wave to the stick man, she left the saloon. The ocean crashed and spread. It made the sand a different color. It left bubbles in its wake. The ocean always seemed capable of teaching a lesson, but really it was just busy water. It didn't know you from anyone. It had never walked the streets. It hadn't started out a baby or gone to school. The sea had a lot living in it, a lot riding on it, but really it just washed itself and sounded independent.

The girl who wrote this isJo. At fifteen years, Jo is very tall, thin, and brown, and reminds one of a colt, for she never seems to know what to do with her long limbs, which are very much in her way. She has a decided mouth, a comical nose, and sharp, gray eyes, which appear to see everything. Her long, thick hair is her one beauty, but it is usually bundled into a net, to be out of her way.

Elizabeth, or Beth, as everyone calls her, is a rosy, smooth-haired, bright-eyed girl of thirteen, with a shy manner, a timid voice, and a peaceful expression which is seldom disturbed. Her father calls her 'Little Miss Tranquility' and the name suits her excellently, for she seems to live in a happy world of her own, only venturing out to meet the few whom she trusts and loves.

Amy, though the youngest, is a most important person, in her own opinion at least. A regular snow maiden with blue eyes and yellow hair curling on her shoulders, pale and slender, she always carries herself like a young lady mindful of her manners. What the characters of the four sisters are we will leave to be found out.

These are the popular sisters from Louisa May Alcott's widely read *Little Women*. Alcott was born in Germantown, Pennsylvania to Abigail May and Bronson Alcott in 1812. Bronson Alcott was a teacher known for his methods. He emphasized conversation and encouraged questioning. "Who is 'four'?" he might ask during a math lesson. "Would an eight be able to put up two fours, if the fours had traveled a long ways and were in need of board?" He was playful, famously letting a chicken loose in the school room to get the pupils' attention. His philosophical teachings have been criticized as inconsistent, hazy and abrupt. The conservative Andrew Norton once said Bronson took the work of "Plato, Kant, and Coleridge and churned them [*sic*] into butter."

In 1840, the Alcotts moved to Concord where prominent American author and close friend Ralph Waldo Emerson helped the family set up. Louisa acted out plays with her sisters and went on nature walks with Henry

David Thoreau. Bronson wished to further his beliefs in transcendentalism and bring his daughters a greater understanding of nature. In 1843, the Alcott family took part in a failed experimental commune. The fruit crop was not what they predicted. The Alcott sisters sobbed they were so sick of hymns and mock battles.

One summer, Louisa had a crush on the shadow of a tree. She was appreciative of lace. Growing up, her best friend was a spoon! She praised all objects, even shoddily-made ones. She did not condescend to animals. She felt most herself in the midst of a long hot bath. Once, she attempted to sew a butterfly's broken wing back together, but the operation failed.

She wrote poems and got them published under nonsense names. Wiggle M. Jenkins. Sneeze S. Breeze. Many of her friends married, but she remained single. She wrote and wrote. She'd think she had nothing left, and then she'd squeeze out another sentence.

Louisa May might have been a lesbian or an intellectual. Her book *Moods* was a precursor to lava lamps. A known civil rights and women's rights advocate, Louisa installed the first washroom in the Underground Railroad. She had a bout of bad luck and dropped a very expensive jar of jam. Some say her sisters never forgave her. While other women were out dancing and spending money in Europe, Louisa was blowing her parents' noses.

Her overnight success with *Little Women* was a shock to the nation. She did cartwheels across a field. Her town was alarmed by the news. The grocer watched her stiffly, unable to make small talk. The librarian got teary-eyed whenever Louisa stopped by. Louisa wrote *Little Men* but it was less fun than she'd thought. Glumly, she swept her house.

The Boston Review quoted her as saying that she'd "fallen in love with so many pretty girls and never once the least bit with any man." But this was before she met the town sheriff. The Sheriff was great. It was like running into a wall if you ran into his chest. He thought Louisa was really funny. She was used to living in a weird dream world, like Emily Dickinson and other ancient girl authors. Once, when she was drunk, Louisa told a Shaman that enlightenment "was bullshit." And she was right.

Louisa wore a lot of layers. The Sheriff made her understand how sexy she was naked. She was used to being a tomboy and a shut-in. She didn't realize she could be those things, but also a really sexy woman, and also an adventurer like Jo from *Little Women*. Louisa and the Sheriff went square dancing and didn't care if they messed up. They hustled pool at the pub. Louisa still wrote stories, but the Sheriff was her main priority. And he still was a Sheriff, but a lot of the time he was just thinking about Louisa and what an original she was.

All his friends thought he was insane, but once they spent time with Louisa they saw she was smart in a spontaneous, natural way, not just a facts way. And she wasn't the normal kind of pretty, she was peculiar.

One day, Louisa was out in the fields with the Sheriff and he was showing her how to shoot a gun, but she was afraid to hold it. He said that Jo wouldn't be afraid to hold a gun and he was right. Louisa laughed her melodious laugh, took the gun and held it. She smiled at the Sheriff because she had finally fallen in love. It was so much more amazing than she'd thought. She had never thought loving a man could outdo being friends with a bunch of eclectic eccentric women, but here she was, in the middle of it, happily proven wrong. The flies in the field chased each other. The sun watched them from behind mountains. Louisa sneezed and her fingers clenched the trigger and the Sheriff was shot in the heart! Down he went like a horse. She fell to his side, mortified, and he held her laughing. He told her he forgave her and he loved her, and she cried and cried and he laughed and he died.

It took Louisa her life to get over her only love. She devoted herself fully to her family and her writing. She wrote letters to women all over the country. Sometimes, she arranged food in a pleasing shape on a plate. Other times, she ate it from the pot. She kept pets and when each died, grimly got another. She sat. She waited. She thought. For years, she wrote an autobiography with flourishes and new additions. In this autobiography, she cared for a lamb named Noelle. She was in a silent movie. When she was finished, she didn't want to stop working. She began the laborious task of typesetting the book. Long ago, she'd inherited a press and had never before printed from it. Using the old type and new ink, she laid out each page. She made only one copy. It took her half a year. Then she drove to town to get it bound. On the day her book was in its complete state, she read it cover to cover. It is extravagant to read a book all about oneself. Louisa felt vain and excited, and then she forgot about it.

Readers, I am that book. My cover is linen and worn. I am 149 pages in total. I am well over a hundred years old. I am positive I am worth a lot of money. Presently, I am squished between others in a rare books collection. I cannot understand spoken language, so the chatter of my collectors is as illuminating as a baby's babble. This could be any country. Nevertheless, I have arrived at some assumptions of this grand room. I sense carpeting. I believe there to be a loud, clinking (grandfather?) clock, for I can sense even intervals, and have no heartbeat to speak of.

I sit next to a first edition copy of *The Great Gatsby*, and it's been sleeping since I got here. I have read that book fifty times since my arrival! I am an avid reader. Many books don't care about reading. Hoards of books are incapable of reading even themselves.

I have read so many books. I'm wild about Nabokov. I admire Cheever. I am not a fan of Latin American fiction. I dislike Kerouac and the other deadbeats. Tolstoy I adore. Henry James, a genius. Early encyclopedias have implemented me with a foundation and overview of the world. Dictionaries have distilled scores of definitions and obscure usages. When there are no books of value to occupy me, I read myself. I know precisely every word.

There was a whole decade I got bored. I just sat there. I did not read. We might call what I did 'meditating,' but, readers, that would be dressing it up. I was surrounded by slick covers of paperback reprints. I had little inclination to be. Then one day, a reader spoke aloud to me. I cannot distinguish sound into words. To me, it was just a mumbling vibration, but I felt this reader was imploring of me. How I struggled to speak back! My binding made a crack, but that is all, my friends.

My life lacks movement, interaction, and event. But I do not expect these things of it. As a life, mine is vicarious, but I suspect most are. It is seldom a book is exposed to the outdoors. A book must study nature from other books and accept that it has been shelved in an artificial environment, and, likely, it will stay there.

More than anything, I desire to attend a symphony. A zoo would be amusing. I can summon little interest in sports contests, but a botanical garden would certainly be educational. I'm quite sure I have a unique perspective. I imagine I'd teach. I'd teach at the University, but summers I'd travel and paint. I'd keep my shape. Frankly, I do not crave a body. A face is intriguing, how it moves and learns, develops, displays, but the mouth has always seemed messy to me. Hair, I imagine to be a chore.

The Jon Lennin Xperience

Jason still read actual books. He was skeptical of internet stars. Someone's cat would suddenly be famous, and Jason wouldn't understand how. His cell phone was basic. His sister was into reality video games and it was all she talked about. She didn't call them games, she called them Xperiences.

"I got to a funny part in 'Dating Kanye,'" she told Jason. "I was tired and snuggling on him, and he asked me which I liked better, dinner or lunch? Well, I was exhausted and happy and I didn't say anything, just snuggled, so he Tweeted the question and immediately got 400 responses!"

Jason liked old things. Baseball, newspapers, rock and roll. He liked going to the post office. For his birthday, his sister got him an unreleased Beatles Xperience and it stayed in his sock drawer, a computer chip in a ziplock bag. They lived together off her money. In high school, she had serendipitously created the popular phone app *Fun Face*.

After *Fun Face* was sold, they moved away from their parents and for two years tried different cities until settling in a lonely loft space in Brooklyn that Jason thought was ruining his life. He took history classes at the New School and played chess in the park against men he was afraid of. His sister ran around museums and had boyfriends and practiced her lousy pool game in bars. After *Fun Face*, no one could tell her what to do. She could buy herself into anything.

Jason was older than his sister, but it no longer felt like an advantage. Somehow he had fallen distractedly behind. The few relationships he had were brief and he'd never been able to give a girl an orgasm. He had even read articles on how. It was a major character flaw of his, he felt. It made him nervous about the rest of his life. Guys in jumpsuits did cool routines in the subway and Jason was paralyzed over whether to give them money.

Sometimes he went out to bars with an acquaintance from his class, but the music was so processed. "It sounds like a baby swallowed a synthesizer!" he said, but Blake did not react. Jason watched people play laser pool. All the girls he met were strangers.

While Jason lifted weights in his room, his sister virtually dated the rap star Kanye West. Other girls across the country were doing the same. Jason walked into the kitchen/dining room/rec room (it was all one crazy mess), and saw his sister talking to Kanye at a restaurant.

"Hi, Jason!" she said, in a voice he'd heard around all her boyfriends. She wore the tight gloves with sensors.

"Hey."

"Move in closer so you can be here."

Kanye was huge on the wall. His sister was there too. The scene did look very real, but dreamy like a Pixar movie. Some spaghetti sauce had even stained the white tablecloth where they were eating.

"Can you taste that?" asked Jason. His sister's spaghetti played in spirals around her fork and spoon.

"No, not really."

Kanye looked at his sister with dewy, rendered eyes.

Jason got a job scanning old newspaper articles into computers at a library. His time split nicely between history classes and this newspaper job, and though he still didn't have any good friends, the city bummed him out less. He spent his free time in Central Park, feeling good about trees, feeling left out by trees, watching people play frisbee. His sister was having trouble with Kanye and often he came home to them fighting in Kanye's flashy apartment. One night, Kanye had left and Jason's sister remained, wandering. She shut the game off with her foot. "He's being an idiot. It keeps ending. Every way I try it. I keep resetting to earlier levels, but it doesn't matter." She looked helpless and wild.

"I bet that's just how the game ends. With the relationship over," Jason said. "They don't want girls to spend the rest of their lives in this game." *Did they?*

"I know. Maybe. I hadn't felt like that about someone in a long time." She took a computer chip out of the game machine. "This is him."

"You should date someone where you can taste the food."

She gradually let go of Kanye. She and Jason ordered pizzas and played cards. The loft no longer felt like a trap to Jason. The ceilings were high with possibility, the extra air gave him ideas. On paper, he drew out the brief timeline of his life. He wrote letters to old high school friends.

His sister was pretty and social; it wasn't long before she had a new boyfriend. Ryan was an amateur boxer/ website creator. They hung out in the living room playing boxing Xperiences. Then she was never around, always at Ryan's, and the loft again greeted Jason in an empty way. He was putting away laundry when he found the ziplock bag and examined the computer chip. Video games had gotten so small. He set it on the kitchen table and stared at it while he ate his meals. He used it to reflect dizzy spots of sun. He pretended it could blow up the world.

Jason was reluctant. The bag was labeled *Jon Lennin Xperience* in smudged marker. Why had they spelled John wrong? Was it mistranslated? He held the chip up to one eye. It looked like a bad little space town. It took him awhile to fit it in the game machine. He switched it on and held the controller.

It was a scene of buildings. It seemed irrelevant. The buildings were computer generated with the same strange glow from the Kanye game. A flock of birds flew by and it was stunning. The buildings were so real (each brick!). Light refracted off water-droplets clinging to a window's screen. Then, the scene dissolved into rolling grassy fields, ancient Japanese cities. An instrumental Beatles medley played and Jason felt moved in an embarrassing, immediate way. Giraffes swayed in a jungle. The Beatles ran through the scenes and it really looked like them. Alive like them.

For a while, he only watched the intro. He'd shut off the game at the menu screen and leave for Manhattan with a good feeling in his face. A person heat. He didn't tell his sister. He'd found an easier way to exist and it wasn't illegal.

He wrote his parents an enthusiastic postcard but didn't mention John Lennon. Jon Lennon. Jon Lennin. Maybe that was a copyright issue. He'd always loved the Beatles, it was the first music he'd heard. It was family car music. He'd never had to grow out of it. He could play 'Norwegian Wood' on the guitar and 'Blackbird.'

He memorized the opening sequence: the sudden descent of the birds, the wink Ringo gave before diving into a glimmering pool. (And the alternate version: George sharing an ice cream with Paul.) One day lingering at the menu screen, Jason just went for it.

Sometimes he was Jon looking out at the world, sometimes he was behind glass at the recording studio. He was Ringo once, searching a mansion for his missing drumstick. He saw Paul naked in the shower laughing. He spoke into the controller and usually people responded. He was the car driving them down the street.

He learned to use his sister's video guitar and the sensey-gloves and wore her dimension glasses. It was insane. Jason would pause the game to eat quick meals of anything then rush back to the game.

They jammed on expensive guitars on someone's balcony.

"Hey Jon! Check this out," Paul played a predictable riff.

Jason played it back and made it better.

Occasionally, he could switch point-of-view by pressing the select button, but usually he was locked. There was no manual, but pressing A and B simultaneously brought up a hints screen that sometimes had background or tutorials. There were levels. He could save his progress. Some of the levels were so long he forgot he was in one.

One night, instead of showing up to his concert, Jason dragged Jon to a dock and watched boats. The wind swept Jon's hair across his glasses. Jason pressed Y + L to search his pockets. A box showed up at the side of the scene that taught Jason to smoke with the X and Y buttons. A pretty girl walked over to him and was rude. Jason carefully climbed Jon down the dock into the water. The sensey gloves were heavy as he swam Jon around. It felt odd. When he dragged Jon back on the dock, there was a small crowd and he was surprised to have passed the level.

Jason's sister was glad he was finally playing. "Great graphics," she said, stopping by for clothes. She gave him a mysterious look. "Hey, I met this girl I want to set you up with!"

"I don't know. Maybe in a few months."

She laughed at him and went back to her boyfriend. Jason was Jon, looking at everything he saw.

It felt good to sing with the band. The lyrics were already memorized. He sang them while a little dot ran the score, marking his pitch. He skipped his New School classes. He scanned newspaper in a haze.

Jon spent whole days with photographers and was interviewed. He went sailing with George and his family. There were button combinations for everything. Jason opened a beer, made the peace sign, cleaned his glasses. He drove cars, restrung guitars, dined with celebrities. Jason helped Jon eat the food and then paused it to eat a rushed meal of rice and ketchup.

When the next level started, Yoko was already in the picture. Everything was going so fast! Jason hadn't even met Cynthia, Lennin's first wife (though once Julian had called on the phone and he hadn't known what to say). He'd been waiting so long for a real girlfriend, what a loss not to see it evolve! Devastated, he skipped Jon's recording session. He wandered around Jon's New York ignoring people. He took Jon into a restaurant and ate plates and plates of meaningless food. When he took Jon back to his apartment, the door was open and Yoko walked out in his old bathrobe. "The first man, my strength."

She had rearranged everything in a far more suiting way.

Her cheeks were enormous and warm. She nestled against him and he carried her to the couch.

"I moved the couch to where it could see better," she said.

"I know. I saw. I love it. I love you."

He had never said that before.

Yoko lay naked on the bed. Jason put on one of her albums and she laughed. Her laugh was like something he'd heard at the zoo once that had made him want to go back. They kissed and Yoko ran her hands over his back. "Love man, sexy Jon, double love." He tried it back, this poem language, it made her laugh. He put a hand on her butt and she didn't stop him. As she teased him and spread her legs, Jason realized he'd have to get her off to get to the next level.

He tried to get a tutorial, but there was none.

"What's wrong, Jon?"

He paused it.

He looked out his huge windows at the rooftops below, the city across the river, the clouds in the weather. The video game was stupid. He turned away from it and did some stretches. He tried to lift weights, but he had gotten bad again. He went off to his room for no reason.

His bed was the same bed he'd had growing up. It was unmade. On his dresser, an old corded landline phone sat next to a box TV. His sister called it "The Museum." There were some old cassettes and a lava lamp too. He pushed back all the books in his bookcase. Normally, video games didn't need you to do this. He had played some growing up and none were anything like this. But he was good at the Xperience. His quick learning of button combinations had helped him. He was at level 22. He was a good Jon.

He unpaused the game. He slid on the gloves and spoke into the controller. "You look very beautiful, Yoko."

She curled around to kiss him and he kissed back. He moved his glove down and stroked her belly and her thighs. "You look like a mermaid," he said, "an actual mermaid, with legs." She laughed and the A button activated Jon's fingers.

The view scrolled to Yoko's vagina. He could tilt the controller and see her face, but it was blurry. The vagina looked very real. All the flaps made Jason nervous. He pressed Y + X and Yoko made a low noise. He reached up toward her breast, but could not reach. He continued pressing Y + X and watched Jon's hands move on Yoko. It was going good. She wiggled closer and he pressed up + AA and she yelled "Ow!" Jason quickly turned off the game. He was trapped again in the huge apartment. He threw down the sweaty sensey gloves. Painted pipes wound above him. He got his keys and left.

He took off jogging, but felt awkward. People stared. They could tell he was a bad runner. He ran past them. He was hungry. He ate a hotdog at a stand. Food! Wind! After his sister ended it with Kanye, she'd felt a new appreciation of actual life. He felt that and cursed the game, but he loved the game. It wasn't a stupid game. It wasn't a game at all.

The park was crowded in a good way. He took his phone out and called his sister. She answered immediately.

"Hey! I was just talking about you!"

"Why?"

"I'm out with Ryan and Jessica! Jessica is the girl I want you to meet."

He could hear laughter in the background, probably Jessica's, he thought.

He met up with them in the Lower East Side. His sister's boyfriend shook his hand as if there were something deep and understood between them. Jessica wasn't bad looking. His sister got up to give Jason her seat so he could sit next to Jessica. She laughed when he sat down.

Jason ate his food eagerly, "like a homeless person!" they teased him. His sister told glorified versions of stories from their childhood. The famous one with Jason climbing a huge tree, refusing to come down, and his sister trying to saw through it. Jessica was half-Jewish half-Muslim and she talked about why that was complicated. His sister made bad jokes and they all took turns making fun of her. Jason felt relieved to be around people.

He and Jessica had a good laugh over *Fun Face* and the young cult surrounding it. Jessica was smarter than he had originally thought. She had studied all over the world. It turned out they had been to the same hostel in Berlin. They talked about all the dog shit in Berlin. Her eyelids fluttered when she laughed, and he decided he liked it. They talked about old musicians no one knew about. She knew who Leadbelly was, which impressed him. Talking with her invigorated him and he itched to run home and play the Xperience.

Jessica bumped into him as they walked out and he could tell by his sister's lit-up face he was supposed to hold Jessica's hand or something, get her number. And he would have, normally, a few months ago, but he had the eerie feeling that Yoko was waiting for him, at home in the loft, and she was an *icon*, who knew *him*! who *loved* him! and he began to feel unsure about wasting his whole night with Jessica, who wasn't going anywhere. She'd be around next week, next month, another time. Thinking about the Xperience he felt so bold that he kissed this Jessica, full on, in front of his sister and her boyfriend, then blushing, ran from the kiss and ducked into the subway.

At the loft he threw his sweatshirt on the floor. He took off his jeans. He pulled down his boxers. Wearing only socks, he walked over to the game. He was a famous musician. He probably had a great body. He started from an earlier level. He was in Paris with the band. He was cold and put his clothes back on. He listened to Ringo talk to Mick Jagger, but Jason was thinking about how once on TV he'd seen a big fish that looked like Yoko, this feminine catfish. He wouldn't try to explain it.

When he got Yoko on the bed, they kissed and rolled around and Jason got Jon's hand going. He did the button combination for smoking and Yoko liked that. He mumbled nonsense into the controller. He did the button combinations Jon used on his guitars. Yoko was making noise. He started whispering to her about the catfish. He couldn't help it. She laughed. His hands hurt. He wanted to put his face in it but he couldn't. It was wide open. It was beautiful. Was it from a photograph? He watched it as he touched it. He kept at his button combinations. He did the one for rewinding a record, the one for waving goodbye. He was afraid he was going to break the controller. He wasn't afraid of anything. His gloved hand touched her thighs, he reached her breast. She was loud. He was pretty sure people could hear from the street. The controller was warm and everything narrowed onto Yoko. Then she let out an amazing sound, like a trumpet dying. The wall fluctuated color. Yoko whispered something in lazy Japanese and the game announced completion of the level.

Jason stared long in the mirror at Jon. He was growing a beard and it was going well. He knew all the combinations, he could rub his eyes, tuck his hair under his ears. His sister kept calling him, but he couldn't stop now. He made pancakes in the kitchen with Yoko. Sean had showed up in level 25. Jason was a father.

They were living post-Beatles, in a long level of daily life. Loving Yoko, feeding Sean. Jason felt fully immersed. He wrote songs that were not part of the level. He had Jon-thoughts about love and humans. He had them even on pause, while getting ready for bed. He had it matched up. He would get Jon into bed and press *sleep* and then he'd get himself into bed. In the morning, there was Yoko and Sean waiting on the wall.

In the end he had to kill Jon. Of course he didn't want to! It was deranged, unfair. Level 27 started off not as Jon, in a tiny bedroom. There was no mirror for Jason to see who he was stuck in. There was a gun under the bed. The door was locked until he picked up the gun. The window was locked. This character's only control was pulling the trigger.

He reset it back a level. He got Yoko off (it was easy now) and laced his shoes. He'd forgotten to put on pants and Yoko laughed. "Let's just stay here!" Jason said.

"No," she insisted, "we have to go to the studio!"

It always went like that. If he dawdled too long the game would freeze and he would have to shut it off and reset it.

Jason paced in the small room. There were loads of Beatles records, but no way to play them. Who was this asshole? Even in this tense situation, Jason marveled at the Xperience. There were cat scratches on the bedposts and real wood grain on the floor. Jason walked up to the desk, but all his fingers could do was pull a trigger. If he held the gun he could walk out the door, but once he got to the hallway, he felt nervous and walked back into the room. He fired the gun and it went off, shot a bullet in the wall and he watched the huge puff of plaster. He tried to shoot his foot, but it would only shoot the floor around his foot.

He shot up the roof, but there was no sky. He shot the records and the pillow. The gun was unlimited. Eventually, a nondescript woman opened the door. "Are you missing your map?" she asked mechanically. Time hadn't been spent on her face. Her eyes were dots. Her mouth, a slot. "It's right here," she said, picking a paper from the floor and handing it to him. "Here," she said and left.

Jason looked at the map. He could not stop this. He walked into the hallway and out the door. He had never played a more twisted game. There was a yellow line he followed. Why couldn't he stay as Jon? He'd rather get shot then shoot. He'd definitely rather that. He considered quitting. He was at the very end, and the end was so fucked up, it wasn't like being a soundman for one level, for a concert level, this was chilly and dark. He thought about Jessica and all the other warm-blooded girls, the people on the street hearing Yoko's orgasms. He followed the yellow line.

It was so unrealistic, the gun in clear sight. This wasn't how it had been. He wanted a cigarette, in the game, but he wasn't Jon. He was some freak who only had one control. He considered stopping the game to get an actual cigarette. Nonsense. He approached Central Park. He followed the line. He got to the point. He waited. He shot at cars and trees and no one did anything. An unlimited gun! Glass broke like how glass did, car tires ran flat when he hit them. A tree just took the bullets, absorbed them, did nothing.

Jon and Yoko got out of a limo and Jason put the gun on them. The gun traced them shakily. A vibration in his gloves made him twitch, the wall brightened white and he shot Yoko, it was a mistake! the whole thing was wrong! but the bullet ran through her not touching. Jon was stalled in place and Jason's face got hot, why was this his responsibility, this stupid world! The glove shook, the wall went white. He shot Lennin and he fell. There was blood and Yoko screamed and Jason pressed select select select and switched to Yoko whose view was dripping tears, and select into Jon whose view was pavement, and the medley started up again, the view soared away, he felt such disappointment, he was being forced out of the experience! But the medley continued, and won him over. Screen shots from the game flashed on the wall, and it was nice sort of, it was sad, and then there were all the names of strangers who had made the game, loads and loads of Asian people, a few Americans too, the meaningless names of animators, assistants, advisors, interns, actors, researchers, archivists, singers, fabricators, programmers, designers, musicians, producers, lawyers. It kept going. It reached the end. It was around 9:00.

The Totems Are Grand

Afternoons find me slow in the bedroom, stiff listening to a woman working towards orgasm. The sounds are pretty animal ones. I don't put music on. I'm always rooting for the woman, any woman. Hers takes her to a place she wants to explain.

Grandma was on her way dying, there was nothing to do. I poked around my room. Tried to invent new kinds of praying. Got naked. Did jumping jacks. I found an ant. Wondered, should I put it outside or in the garbage? The garbage is easier, but the ant dies. Not today, today it eats garbage. But when the garbage gets put in bigger garbage, the ant will get claustrophobic, die. Outside, the ant might get cold. My cell phone rang; the family had found something to make for Grandma. In the cousins' yard, a bunch of trees just sitting there, doing nothing.

They'd already started when I got there. Hack-saws and chain-saws, milk paint. My parents, cousins, aunts, and uncles. Frankie explained as I got out. The dogs wove excitedly around us, dragging sticks. Little Freezy Jane took the knives from the drawer. Bananas wasn't allowed any sharp object, so dug with a spoon in the dirt.

The trees had been gnawed like pencils. I picked up a gouge and mallet and peeled off the price-tags. I didn't immediately carve a face in. A tree is best as is, to brand it—aesthetically questionable, but this tree was a telephone pole without electricity. It was skeleton and bare. Whatever relationship the other trees had with this one was gone; it needed decoration as a role, to keep it upright, how it preferred. I thought of Grandma and hammered the gouge into the bark, carving a big Jewish star. Fresh wood fell to my shirt, to the grass. And then a five-pointed star, which means Good! or Good Job! I looked at the other tree carvers. My parents were sharpening the chisels. My brother was hauling away the scraps so Frankie could cut the grass. I liked seeing us on the front lawn together. Like we had made the world small on purpose. I looked at them teary-eyed, but a family you can't see all at once. A family runs at different intervals, though a family tree would have you believe everyone stays, waiting the whole thing out.

"Get some saw dust in those tears!" My uncle said, wailing his chainsaw through a tree branch. Cousin Milt poured beer over his carving. Usually we worked apart in businesses and schools, towards our own popularity and successes. If we ever made a great feast, we ate it immediately. We'd never left anything behind besides pictures, but now how the trees stood, noble and armless!

Delirious from teamwork, we built fires with the extra wood, pitched tents among the totems. Eyes closed pretending sleep, we imagined we were a tribe. These were skinny totems, sure, but in modern times one must comply. It was okay to cut up trees. We recycled. Dying gets everyone feeling alive. If you don't distribute the energies right, a family loses money to gambling, affection to television, togetherness to private mulling.

The totems came along quickly. We used ladders and neighbors' ladders, platforms built between two ladders. Spotters and runners. Milt hit his mouth like an Indian and we laughed. We carved smiley faces, an octopus, fish shapes, a gorilla signing sign language, a man, a woman, a baby/zombie, jack-o-lantern faces, plus numerous ballpoint pen drawings: the twin towers falling, ice cream sundaes, ships with cargo, peace signs, Mercedes signs, and Pearl Jam lyrics.

In the night, dogs barked to other dogs. Tough cars made fast noises. In the morning, Bananas held Freezy's ponytail to her mouth, "Can you hear what I am saying? I am saying 'I am saying.'" I put off going back to work. We gave this event a capital letter. Every Grandma-thought we coupled with this new thought: the Event! the Monument! Our thoughts left us at a happy dead end, the inevitable celebration of Woman and Monument. Feelings finally turned three-dimensional! We only discussed this at night, with the totems a safe distance back, glowing from the fire. Was it wrong to burn a tree's arms in front of an armless tree? We laughed at Bananas' question, but it troubled us. What about the flipside? There was always the flipside. You had to remind yourself. Oh yeah, the dying, we'd remember. Wood cut into a box. But how great the totems looked sticking up from the lawn!

One night, Freezy explained ghosts. "Look Bananas, here we are all bodies, each with a personality. But what if our body got so sick it never moved again and our personality floated out?" Freezy made her hands like a butterfly flying around her. "If there weren't such strict rules of science, I would visit the dead world." Frankie rolled his eyes. It was past all bedtimes. Freezy danced around the kitchen. "Let there be ghosts!" she whispered into the knife-fork-and-spoon drawer. "Let there be ghosts!" to the totems through the window.

Milt told a ghost story about a plane crash during a war. The pilot was covered with flames and there was no water. Then the younger cousins told ones they'd heard. Most of the stories had the sad ghost trying to creep back into life, the paradise of the bodies. They just wanted to play a small part. They were lonely. They knew nothing bad could really happen to them because something already had.

The totems were almost complete. Frankie added a sports part with a carved football and hockey puck, including an actual baseball bat nailed on. I wrote a poem in Sharpie and dug out our initials at the base of the totems. My mother finished a carving of Grandma while my aunt sawed out a representation of god. Freezy told me that god was life and life was blood in bodies (human life at least) and that if we had bodies, well, then we could forget it, all the looking for god and calling out to him (or her or it). "He's right here, Stupid!" she said, jabbing me in the chest.

Grandma hated the totems. The kids were trying tricks on their jump ropes, hurting each other with glee, when Grandma stepped out of the car service. "How I hate public art," she declared grandly. We looked at the smiley faces gouged in, the stickers Bananas had spared from her collection. Grandma stuck a high heel in the recently cut grass. "Isn't life lively enough?" Stray blades stuck on her patent leather. Her left heel impatiently brushed off her right. "Life was *certainly* lively enough!" She glanced at the totems, then at her outfit with approval—blue ultrasuede vest and pants, fox fur trim, and a huge turquoise pendant that cooled her heart. She looked each of us in the face. "There were so many textures," she said to Freezy Jane. "The sky was always changing. If for one minute it was all one shade of blue-grey, then a pack of birds would fly right through it, or an airplane, always!" Our eyes settled on the grinning Mickey Mouse head Milt was proud of, the bright poster paint where Freezy could reach. How come it looked so good when the Indians did it? She paced unsteadily. Her heels were covered in cut grass. She stuck a finger in a totem groove. "That was my favorite part, how even the sky never looked solid." Jump ropes fell around sneakers.

Grandma put her purse down. "The kids were beautiful in their selfishness. The little possessions they held in shelves, delicate things they were not afraid to break and they broke them. All dogs played in this grassy area in the middle." She motioned to the long yard between the house and the road. "Life was wide and open. Trees were for climbing, spiders made crazy houses." Grandma leaned towards me and whispered, "Sex will take you down. You will like it, but it will trick you. Your stomach will egg out, love and time braiding unconsciously together, the years collecting in a net. Wearily you will have to keep on, even when you are half-full of birthdays."

Grandma wandered back over to one of the totems. She leaned against it for support. "What's this?" Freezy showed her the part that was Freezy's belongings hot-glued on. "Your machine!" Grandma gasped touching the mini-iPod. This was the machine that waited on Freezy's napkin while dinner was in session, that teachers confiscated daily and gave back at the bell.

Freezy crawled up one of the ladders and declared, "Forget about money and things that take up place! I mean *space*. This stuff is nothing compared to a real person." Her words like ribbon, her whole life in a fat nine years, "The totems are grand! We are having so much fun!" She looked at Grandma leaning against the totem and continued bravely, "In the end, the END, the end will pass as quick as the Super Bowl does. Really quick like the Super Bowl dies. Like the Super Bowl does, earlier each year. Trash overflowing places for trash. My bath overflowing and ruining my bath." Freezy sat down on the ladder. We looked expectantly at Grandma.

"What are you all waiting for? An alien ship to touch down and take me away? The kids should be in school." Bananas hid behind Milt. Grandma slung her purse strap over her shoulder. "I love all of you. Today is just a day. I'll miss you. If you felt you had to hack up the trees, well, then I'm sorry for the animals that used to live there." She smiled wanly at us, touched the mini-iPod's blank face, and then rode home in her car service.

We sat on the front lawn. Not Indian-style like we'd been doing. This time we made sure not to sit that way, except Bananas. Bananas always sat that way. We considered cutting down the totems. They were weird. Here it was, the flipside. "Don't listen to Grandma,"

Bananas said, "she just felt left out. We should have invited her and asked her what she wanted to do." Neighbors watched us from their windows. I looked at online plane tickets. We agreed to sleep inside and evaluate the totems in the morning. We didn't realize they'd be evaluated every morning. By cars and neighbors, by the original tree carvers, pecked at by birds, traveled by ants. You cannot remove a monument, everything moves around it.

Grandma's earlier style of dying turned into a more advanced, un-stylish dying. We took turns waiting with her. "I'm not sure which I'm more attracted to," I said to her, "boys or dogs." She was only ten percent awake. I said, "I keep crashing my car, just so me and Dad will have something to fix." She opened one eye and then snapped it shut. I poked at the little pills in their order. "They got rid of Florida," I told her, "you can't move there now. Just broke it off."

Two girls my age came in and started getting involved. Hospice, the ones who brought the bed with a remote control. They were dressed in lace and black. They asked, "What have you done to the pills?" I had arranged the week's medicine in color order. The yellows to red to blue. The girls scowled. They had black nail polish. I excused myself and walked into Grandma's bathroom. "Mom," I whispered to my phone, "what kind of association is this? I swear they are two *goth* girls." I tried to explain goth to Mom over the phone, "Like Shakespeare?" she asked. "No, different," I said, "They love death. Like their whole life is to prepare and get used to death, to, and, and to dress dramatic. They avoid certain things. They only have a few friends. Usually. They hate their parents, usually."

I caught one hospice girl looking through the closet and pushed the sliding door shut. "She's not dead yet," I said, "Plus, you aren't getting those clothes for your thrift store! I'm going to get those clothes and be my own living ghost. Grand! In the old style! You get it?" These girls should not have been touching Grandma. Each moment of her was waning. I looked at her for resemblance. A life is enormous.

These girls were like people in line at the grocery store. Getting unfamiliar foods. Foods I never buy. The other girl was poised above Grandma. "Don't do anything weird," I said.

"I'm not," said the girl.

I reorganized the nightstand how me and Grandma liked it. I sat down in my waiting chair and stared into the black eyes of the girls, "Don't try to manipulate souls. We are both solid Jews in here. We don't believe in anything but life."

My mother made the girls leave. I relaxed. I caught a show on television about inner city kids learning to ballroom dance. I cried. I watched the preview channel.

All the things I could have been watching. I watched the 7:00 box move up into 6:30. 7:30 into 7:00.

Grandma tries to regain strength by lying still, not eating, by acting dead. I am waiting for when she will sit up weakly and become brilliant, channeling wisdom of relatives passed. She will tell of family who lived in Russia, eating grass, wearing seven skirts. She will tell secrets way deeper than religious texts. Almost every book I've ever read is better than a religious text. It's like they didn't even try. She stirs in her bed. I sit up straight and hold my breath. "Who is sick?" she asks me. She can tell someone is.

The Kid

A t the end of the summer, the kid was assigned some
drop-offs down south. The girl went with him because
now she lived with the kid in his basement. She lived in
his life. He left the girl with the dog in motels, flipping channels.
He drove the speed limit and came to full stops at stop signs.
The drugs were in plastic bags in the backseat seat lining. On
the last drop-off, he left the dog at the motel, but took the girl
with him, even though he wasn't supposed to. He had a girl.

The kid had a mother that couldn't stop crying. The girl had
a stepfather she hated. Before the kid, she went out with older
guys she met working at the mini mart. The kid had a freckle
on his penis, so usually avoided girls. The summer before 12th
grade, the girl slept in her car on the kid's street. They knew

each other from math class. He knocked on her window and she let him in and they chewed a whole pack of peppermint Lifesavers, then he took her back to the basement, which was his bedroom. Old Nintendo games littered the floor like headstones. The kid showed the girl his beagle dog, who he was in love with. The girl reached out to pet its head, the beagle stared back unimpressed. It took the dog years to fall in love. The girl could do it in about a month.

It was only a small amount, some guy last minute. They found the apartment easy. The man answered the door shirtless, a few hairs stuck out his low slung pants. There was music and the man took the girl's hand and twirled her like they were dancing. She laughed and looked at the kid. The man took them inside where a woman was sprawled on the couch. He said the name of the kid's brother. He said disgusting things about the woman on the couch. He said that the girl should live in the spare room and that the kid could keep the drugs. The kid didn't laugh, because he never fake laughed. The girl laughed because she was nervous. There was an uneasy space where the kid was not laughing.

The kid went to the bathroom and there was a crystal Buddha above the toilet. The Buddha's eyes glimmered at the kid. Rubies had been used for the eyes. He looked in the mirror and checked on his pimple. Anything inside to set free? Nothing. His hands scratched his scalp looking for the scab. Bathrooms were the only real private time. Even in a car, there are people looking from their cars. In a normal room someone can just walk in whenever. A bedroom with so many socks and sheets and things. But a bathroom is small and hard.

The kid looked into the rubies. What kind of moment was this, with the Buddha in the bathroom? A drip dropped. The Buddha was the bathroom, the non-moments. Peaceful, anxious. The scab the kid usually scratched off wasn't there. He had neglected to scratch it and it had healed. The kid lifted the Buddha into his backpack. He took a little of the drugs and put it in a separate bag in his pocket. The girl had always wanted to try the drug and he had never let her. Then he took a shit in the toilet and looked at it. The shit slowly moved in the water and he left it floating.

The kid's car was a quality one and his skin was white enough. He had a clean record and a nice face. He ran drugs and sometimes stolen things over state lines. The job had been left to him by his older brother who died two summers before. The kid and the girl had fallen into something. Now the boy knew it didn't matter there was a freckle on his penis. The girl liked the kid better than the men from the mini mart, because he got sweet like a baby and held her while they slept. When they awoke, there was a blissful moment of remembering about each other. The girl didn't need to listen to Nine Inch Nails anymore to function. She didn't need anything.

In the living room, the man was showing the girl other Buddhas. Some were marble, some were wood. He said they were always meditating, that some had been meditating for hundreds of years, that he had won them on eBay. The kid gave the drugs and the man gave the money.

The man looked at the kid and the girl. His life was missing a sort of action that used to jump it week to week. No one had punched him out in a long time. He wanted to say something to the kids, but there wasn't anything. At one point, there had been a string of situations. All of a sudden he'd be gunning it on a highway, some guy playing confident on the radio and the confidence would rub onto him. He'd be in a lumber yard with only a vague notion. One minute he'd be saying one thing and the next something else. There was no looking back. Now, all there were were the Buddhas. The Buddhas and the woman. The kids had a lucky stupidness, he thought. The sex they had wasn't even sexy. It was simple, probably. Their worlds were whole like little baseball stadiums— with tiny players playing in little clean uniforms, but getting in fights too sometimes. The little players would get bloody noses, he thought. The woman on the couch made a sound. The man looked wildly at the kid. The kid said nothing.

The girl drove the kid into town and they ate at a restaurant with too much junk stuck on its walls. "Let's just keep the money and never drive back. Let's skip the whole 12th grade," the girl said with her mouth full of hamburger. "Let's live down here." The kid agreed and then they were silent. The kid wasn't sure if he was serious. He knew the girl was, because she would often get a quick idea and then just do it numbly, like there had never been a choice.

Outside by the curb, young street kids wove bamboos into roses. The rain ruined blouses. The kid and the girl walked through a creepy park. Benefit flyers blew in the wind. The kid found a poster that looked like the dog. On each corner was a bent-up kid trying to sell the roses. They walked over broken glass, cigarette butts, and wet bamboo roses, flattened by sneakers, dead on the sidewalk.

Back at the motel, the dog was curled between the beds. The carpet was dark with pee. The kid fumbled with the card key, but the lock was broken. He pushed open the door easily. Giddy with affection, he spotted the dog. He pulled the sleepy beagle into his lap and cooed. The dog yelped back. The kid cooed. Yelp. Coo. Yelp. The girl watched. The kid and dog held each other. "I don't get up on this," she said. The kid pulled his eyes from the dog and smiled at the girl. The dog licked his hand, licked between his fingers. "There's something you two get that I just can't get up on." The kid smoothed the dog's ears. The girl took off her shirt. The dog and kid looked away. She laid on one of the beds. Its thick comforter was wrapped over, trapping the pillow. She took her hair down. The kid left the dog and went to the girl. He pulled the bag out of his pocket. The girl was excited and they kissed. The kid thought of the Buddha and didn't want to think of it, so put his fingers in the girl.

Afterwards, she filled the bath. The water was too hot and cooked their minds empty. The surface was flaked with pubic hairs and bits of dead skin. The girl's thigh rose above it. In the numb heat, their top lips dried to their bottoms, boredom secured.

The dog was barking and that got the kid moving, the water moving, but the girl ignored it and sunk into the boredom. There was a sound and the kid jumped out the tub and pulled his jeans on over his wet legs, over his freckled penis. The knocking shook the girl's heart, but she eased herself up. She started dressing as the door slammed open, the knob wrecking a hole in the wall. The man had the kid by the neck and the woman was laughing. The man had a gun. The woman had one too, and aimed hers at the girl. Backing into the bathroom, the woman pushed towards her until the gun was snug against the girl's head.

The kid was holding the dog in his hands and the man held tight on the kid's neck. The girl laughed. With his other hand, the man opened the kid's Jansport backpack and took out a notebook, balled-up socks, and then the Buddha. The girl stared at the Buddha. The Buddha stared back with eyes of fire. The Buddha had been there meditating, through their sex and their bath. The Buddha was always having a bath.

She could see right through the Buddha because he was crystal. She could see through the kid too, but not the man, the dog, or the woman. She could see through herself because she was inside and outside. The man aimed his gun and shot the Buddha. The woman snickered. The bottom of the Buddha sat there, legs folded on top of legs, still meditating. The top of the Buddha had shattered across the room. A bit of the Buddha was sticking out of the girl's arm. The girl saw it, but didn't move. The Buddha had touched her. It stung.

The man put the gun against the dog's ear. The woman released her trigger guard. The girl could hear the gun against her hair. The kid was hyperventilating. The man told the kid to pick. The girl's clothes weren't on well. The dog licked at the kid's hands and didn't know about the gun. The dog licked the gun. The girl could feel the gun against her hair and her hair against her scalp and how her scalp was covering the rock of her skull. The kid was trembling on the floor. The dog had been a puppy when the kid was a kid and the dog had smooth ears. The girl was the only person the kid had ever had sex with. The girl would laugh after good orgasms. The dog liked to be inside sweatshirts.

The two guns hovered and pushed. The kid wouldn't look at the girl. He kissed and kissed his dog's head. The man whispered something disgusting about the kid's choice. The kid could not choose. The dog always yelped and wagged when he saw the kid. The girl had a nice way of singing along to songs. The dog knew more words than most dogs. The girl couldn't think if there was a more humiliating way to die. She couldn't see through the kid anymore. Only her and the Buddha were clear of anything.

The summer was forced into fall. The kid was back home, but didn't want to start 12th grade. He didn't want to start his sandwich, which lay in tinfoil in front of him. The tattoo gun's needle went in and out with a hum. The shape of a beagle head was being stabbed into his arm. Carefully, fur was added on, and whiskers, a little glimmer in the eyes that made the head come alive. It had been the girl's idea. The kid was crying and couldn't stop. The girl was bored of the crying. The tattoo man pretended not to see.

Iconographic Conventions
of Pre- and Early Renaissance:
Italian Representations of
the Flagellation of Christ

The New Testament offers no specific description of the flagellation of Jesus Christ and very little of the rest of the Passion: Jesus' criminal indictment, subsequent suffering, and execution. Yet this series of events received *massive artistic attention* in the Middle Ages and Early Renaissance, depicted thousands of times with a certain consistency of imagery. Biblical flagellation scenes in painting and sculpture from 1300 A.D. to 1525 A.D. exhibit unmistakable iconographic repetition. Given the lack of source material from which to draw, artists of these centuries heavily borrowed from their peers and predecessors.

Historical coverage of the Passion is slim. In this significant historical void, great artistic liberties could initially be taken as interest in the subject expanded. Someone once decided, for example, that Jesus had been bound to a column and this achieved a thematic resonance with the audiences of the time, encouraging artists to repeat it. Someone decided Christ was slender, his hair gingerly framing his long face. Long like a horse and long like unhappy. Thereafter, artists followed formats that conveyed the message successfully, deviating rarely and then only slightly. No monumental compositional alterations occurred for hundreds of years.

This common practice of formal imitation and borrowing is unremarkable, but as the accumulation of passion-related imagery accelerates through this time period, visual history achieves legitimacy. Passion (from the Latin *patior*, meaning to suffer or to endure) is an emotion of intense, compelling enthusiasm for a person, object, activity or idea. The Passion quotient is used in Thomas Friedman's formula of $CQ + PQ > IQ$. Curiosity plus passion is greater than intelligence.

No description exists. Christ was slender, his hair casually framing his long face. Like a horse's and unhappy. Like a bluesman playing his blues. A mostly empty ketchup, a basset hound looking low with eyelids lower. His chest had some or none hairs. A beard over his cheeks because that was the style back then; *only warriors shaved their beards,* and that was to show how sharp their swords were. That was for fun. Also, it was custom for a cuckold to have a warrior shave his beard, publicly showing his marriage as flawed, an invitation to flaw it further.

Curiosity plus passion is *almost* equal to being smart. E = a Mazda car driving twice as fast. E = Michael Jordan dunking two balls while coughing. God is the closest thing to an all-knowing entity. She indexes over 9.5 *billion* web pages, which is more than any search engine on the web. She sorts through this vast amount of knowledge using her patented PageRank technology. God is virtually everywhere on earth at the same time. With the proliferation of Wi-Fi networks, one will eventually be able to access God.

Through repetition, validity is assumed. The flagellation thus becomes one part of a larger visual narrative, instantly recognizable. Flagellation scenes turn iconic in their thematic compatibility with each other. To see one is to be reminded of others already seen. This repetition strengthens their representation in religious culture. As with the crucifixion, a familiarity close to comfort arises when gazing at a crucifixion painting, knowing absolutely the being being killed will be a white male with a long face and relatively long nose. Nails and blood are optional. Clouds, optional. Weeping women, optional.

Children tend to add a curlicue of smoke upon the addition of a chimney in a drawing of a house. What if all beach scenes had a symmetry of beach umbrellas and a ratio of birds to sky? A formation that urged copying.

In China, there are no curlicues of smoke in children's drawings. Smoke is usually represented by several soft, wavering lines. The sometimes discounted studies of children's drawings have informed larger studies of lifestyle differences. "California coast drawings varied greatly according to the quality of the children's mark-making tools. Wealthy children had the opportunity to mosaic with minerals and a wide variety of artistic plastics, whereas children in poorer neighborhoods stuck to construction paper and in extreme cases, *broken glass.*"

Stick people are not necessarily the child-drawing norm. Studies found young Russian children making "bubble-men," as researchers referred to them. These rounded sketches were thought to originate from the abundance of snowmen during the lengthy, snow-prone winters of the region.

When American college students take their year abroad, there is no one familiar to greet them except a loneliness they outgrew years ago. Friends will be forged like signatures. From this great distance, they will finally be able to see America, from looking around and not finding it. Buildings like cakes instead of Legos. If they go to art museums, they feel anxious. How can one *stand* the exquisitely stunning, divinely magnificent paintings in European cities? Making one nostalgic for the Middle Ages, the early ages, painted so *painfully* there are nowhere strokes, nowhere splatters. It's unnerving to see a scene so deeply actualized in two dimensions, the David in three, appealingly human, the most appealing human, a new ideal to bring home along with the souvenirs.

Viewers find themselves in an anxious daze by the end of these museums. The final floors are skipped or else run through frantically. The way to take these paintings in is to blink them, blur them, to look a little less than needed. Such eye-pleasing two-dimensionals beg to be marred, trashed, exposed in two dimensions. A wad of gum would do it, little circles of spit, a knife to reveal the wall behind it. It has been suggested the Louvre commission some semi-fantastic copies *of good size*, very fine, expert renderings of one of the museum's paintings, perhaps a collaged scene of a few, and hang them near the cafeteria to be mauled and defaced by tourists sick on beauty.

Back to the discussion on David: Michelangelo has set up more than one teenage girl for disappointment. Delicate, arrogant, naturally toned, with big hands to hold, many girls fly home heart-struck, it's true! Flocking to the first curly-haired boy they see, looking more carefully at the football team, too much time in the library, tying the phone cord in knots, settling for a prom date, etc., etc., rooting for Italy in the Olympics. Relative to Jesus, but in a different way. One girl's experience with both was to fall for the David, returning home only to sculpt him out of white chocolate and melt him (*melt him!*) on a hot plate. Then meeting a David and understanding the world's preoccupation with Jesus, see diary entry below:

> *The bluest eye proposal was met by one unknowing boy who had the bluest eyes, winning, generous, butt-perfect, pleasing, spontaneous and breathing, but shy,*

*silly, dillied all down. If Jesus was like that, then all the
more explained.*

If one could suspend knowledge and judgment,
consider Jesus as the kind-hearted high school sweetheart
who dies *tragically in a car crash* (and just two days
before graduation!). A dead boyfriend, as we all know, is
impossible to *get over*, having committed no crime besides
stealing our hearts, etc. Breaking off a relationship with no
one *breaking it off*, this kind of end is very hard to accept,
leaving the left one thinking, *if only* I had driven myself,
if only I hadn't *insisted on ice cream*, if only the weather
had been nicer, or the road had been cleared, or my purse
hadn't been *lazily* draped over the gear shift, *etc*. The
world wants to meet, to speak with, the tragically died-
young, the perpetual. There is no old-aged Lennon, no
middle-aged Cobain. To die young is to stay young, to
keep everyone wanting to stay young with you, to make
them afraid to approach an age you never got to, that you
were supposed to get to first.

In Japan, a young girl published an essay on Cobain's
voice. A rough translation states:

*Cobain's voice houses more than one voice. This magic
of voice is most clearly deciphered on the* Unplugged
*Album. I could find enough levels in Kurt Cobain's
voice to live satisfied, but the rest of my family wasn't
as fortunate.*

The text goes on to question the structural make up of Cobain's throat. Does it contain pebbles or kernels? Would the writer try to communicate with Cobain if he had not left his body behind as evidence? Does one assist a dead musician by covering his songs?

Songs have been covered since the first melody hummed in the presence of another. Monkeys covered songs way before they lost the hair. Adam and Eve used to sing while they had sex in streams. Crickets sure sing similar and leaves have a song, birds, thunder claps are a kind, not so popular or pleasing, but everyone has their music. Different car engines sound good together. An airplane duets nicely with a lawnmower. Music proves one of the most exciting and accessible art forms to cover. A number of literary covers have been produced by a junior high English class, the text only differing in handwriting. Civil War reenactments could be considered covers, but those wars are fake. A cover song holds all qualities that define a song; a cover song is definitely *real*. One can argue, as the text here is about to, a cover version makes a song *more* real, alive even, since changing the form calls attention to the original, shows the song is still identifiable as the song, even with different qualities.

Some turn into dance songs, "Always on My Mind," for instance, sung first by Brenda Lee, popularized by Elvis, then re-covered by Willie Nelson, then turned dance by the Pet Shop Boys. Newly-turned dance covers sound careless, freed from their gloom by immortal beats. These beats keep going after the song has stopped. Beat-making machines have no *off* button. They must be stuffed in pillows, in closets, in sheds, buried in backyards, until the beat is needed once again.

Does a cover unleash the song? One that's been called the best, Hendrix completely outgunning a Dylan original, throwing it far from Bob's scratchy so-so. John Coltrane rescues "My Favourite Things" from the original *The Sound of Music* version. His meandering jazz masterpiece weaves in and out of melody, trilling notes out of control, and all the while the listener has the other prim version in her head. No one sings lyrics in Coltrane's version. They are offered by the song's ghost. Coltrane's melody calls to mind the kittens and string. Then the instruments storm, there are hundreds of cats, way too much string.

Digital appropriation can be a form of 4th dimensional rape, as in the mash-up of Ludacris's "What's Your Fantasy" and Kylie Minogue's "Can't Get You Out of My Head." The combination of the two, referred to as "Can't lick you out of my head," puts Kylie's backing dance beat over Ludacris's dark questioning keyboard, transforming Ludacris's lyrics into a seduction. All that's left of Kylie's voice is her girlish "la-la-la" chorus and it's being used against her. Anonymous assault is common, comparable to Photoshop scandal, the cut and paste from one online chat to another, but *incomparable* to the questionable assault of Kobe Bryant upon Unnamed:

> *We stood right here and started having the you know, the foreplay happened right here ... the hug goodbye thing or whatever ... we just started kissing. I asked her I said you know, she bent over, and walked over on her own free will ... put her foot up here all by herself and if that wasn't consensual ... Did she cry, no ... She didn't cry at all ... I didn't say she slipped off, she just you know removed herself from ... I said she slid off ... Slid off like when uh, that was it and I stood there like this and uh you know, put it back in my pants so you know, that was it no more no nothing ... She kissed goodbye. Boom ... I put my thing back in my pants when I was through and she ... no, she didn't leave, we kissed goodbye, we kissed goodbye*

Other notorious ballers, the Detroit Piston Bad Boys were known for their unforgiving physical style. One of Rick Mahorn's tactics was to foul an opponent after another Piston had already fouled him and the whistle had blown. In a display of poor sportsmanship, they walked off the court, refusing to shake hands with the Bulls after losing to them in the 1991 Eastern Conference Finals.

Legacies leave things behind. The left-behinds transform to the lost. None would know how Christ looked had the villagers not run to their huts inspired. Darwin patterns decorate more than exotic animals. The Toyota Camry slowly morphs to the more luxury look of the Lexus. A prominent Cadillac grill copied on a new Ford. Is this the same thing that gets daughters like mothers? Nowadays, teens are texting their picks for natural selection.

Are Jesus paintings covers of Jesus paintings? Or of Jesus? One can argue *all* portraits as covers, *sunsets covers too*, a day a cover of the last, a year, a century. The USA a cover of England. Football a cover of war. This links everything to a repetitive tradition. Lightning bolts assisted in this game of improvement. Saints no longer hoard ecstasy. iPod nanos spark bedrooms on fire. As Jimi Hendrix writes on a postcard home:

> *Belief comes through electricity. We're playing for our sound to go inside of the soul. You're not going to find it in church. A lot of kids don't find nothing in church. I remember I got thrown out of church because I had the improper clothes on. I had tennis shoes and a suit.*

Dream House

They were so in love that JP switched all his afternoon classes to Missy's schedule. Missy had tried to switch hers, but she had the mean guidance counselor. Everyday JP quickly changed into gym clothes to be the first one waiting outside the girls' locker room. Tying her hair with an elastic, Missy would stroll out with a calmness that had to do with dating JP. In CVS, Missy looked at sex tips in *Cosmo*, trying to become a more adventurous lover. It was always the same tips. "It doesn't feel good there," JP said kindly as she tried to find it again, between the testicles and the anus, the spot magazine people swore by.

Walking down Main Street, it was beautiful weather. "This is the season with most beautiful weather!" JP announced. "All seasons have beautiful weather!" sang Missy and JP did not disagree. Again JP brought up the plans for their dream house.

Recently, they had added a new room, the live butterfly room, inspired by the exhibit at the Natural History Museum. Missy bought an ice cream and they sat on the park bench trading licks. In the vacant lot where the gas station used to be, the middle-school skater kids had set up some jumps and a poorly constructed half-pipe. "How about a planetarium?"

"Yes!" JP took a big lick, blending the chocolate with the vanilla. "Wait, no," he poked Missy in a ticklish place, "now its starting to sound too much like the museum!" She laughed. The skateboards made a nice sound of wheels running over rough ground. The skater kids weren't any older than 5th grade. One of them must have been in elementary school. He wore enormous JNCO cords over his puny legs.

"Do you still think our parents should live underground?" Missy wrinkled her forehead, "Or was that just part of the old plan?" JP put his arm around Missy's shoulder, his hand reaching to brush against her boob.

"Not underground! Their houses will be above-ground, but attached to ours with an underground tunnel!" Missy hoped someone might see the hand on her boob. It wasn't supposed to be there. One of the 5th grade skaters didn't have enough money for pizza so he started to propose dare-devil stunts. "If I skate up that board, then ollie in the air, grab on that bar and do a flip, you have to give me a dollar." Missy discreetly moved her hand to JP's erection, pushing it through his jeans. She stared at the elementary-school skater without seeing him. "Should they live in the same house, or different houses?" She murmured, unsure of what she was saying. JP squeezed her nipple through her shirt, "The same house," he whispered in her ear, then squeezing it once more, "different houses I mean." A cool wind blew on their faces.

The 5th grader did the stunt and landed. No one would give him any dollars. One kid took a penny and threw it at his forehead. The elementary-school skater laughed a silly high-pitched laugh. The laugh echoed in Missy's ears as she stuck her tongue in JP's mouth. JP's mouth was the best place she'd ever been. It was like falling asleep and waking up. Could there be a room in the dream house that would feel like JP's mouth? Oh wait, she could just kiss JP in any of the rooms. Again the calmness filled her body. JP's erection got bigger and with a muscle he had, he made it twitch, butting through his jeans against Missy's hand.

"I bet you can't do that, douchebag!" The 5th grader challenged the elementary-school skater, pushing him into a brick wall. Missy had her finger on the tiny gold zipper that could unzip JP's fly. JP's tongue shoved wildly in her mouth, which she endured, disapproving his methods but relishing his enthusiasm. Once, she had read in the Guinness Book of World Records that two people had once kissed for 3 days straight. Did they sleep with their tongues in each other's mouths? How did they eat? JP's hand held Missy's boob. She had wanted a four-poster bed, but JP had suggested a loft bed because they were cool. One time Missy had seen a movie about a young artist who slept in a loft bed and bathed in a bathtub that was in the center of her apartment. Her apartment was one big room. For curtains the artist had stapled up her wedding dress. She had run out on her wedding to move to New York City. The dream house wasn't going to be in New York City though. There wouldn't be enough space. It wouldn't be feasible.

"Let's add a stain-glass window," Missy said with his tongue in her mouth. She opened one eye and he opened one and they stared at each other like bugs. His finger returned to her nipple and she forgot about the dream house. The elementary-school skater skated up the ramp gaining speed, then tried to jump to the bar, over-shot it, hit his head with a crack, skidding his knees and elbows on the pavement. There was blood on his corduroy JNCOs. The boys crowded around. JP looked at the commotion and Missy felt her mouth empty again, wonderful-JP-tongue having left. JP turned back and was struck by the glazed look of Missy's face. "Of course stain-glass windows, loads of stained glass," he said into her neck. This time she did pull the zipper down. She wriggled her hand in his boxers and felt through the opening, his bare penis! The first time she had touched his penis, it had reminded her of the rubbery legs of barbies. Then she got used to it. Now she thought it felt smooth. Smooth like a baby. Eww, not like a baby! Adults had run over and a man knelt beside the fallen skater. The dare-devil 5th grader was crying. Missy paused her hand to watch this crying. Crying was beautiful too. Especially in the season of good-feeling weather. Crying was like waterfalls. No, not like waterfalls, but it looked like, what did it look like? Crying felt like tired-after-dancing. The elementary-school skater had a bloody face with gravel stuck in it. A part of his head was wet with blood too. The hair was slicked or else missing. "Ewww," Missy could see it with the one eye she opened. Then more adults blocked her view and she turned back to JP. Somehow a little feather, like one from a baby chick had landed in his hair!

If it wasn't past 5, then they could stay out a little longer. Maybe at 5 they would get cheese slices. She nibbled on JP's lip. A siren moaned in the distance. Sirens sounded pretty, like boat language, or like when a plane goes past a rainbow in the sky and makes a special sonic cry. JP took his hand away from her nipple and she remembered again about the house. Maybe if one of the lobbies were open to the winter air, maybe then they could have an ice sculpture. In one of the courtyards. Sometimes, the ice sculpture could be her and JP's initials, another time, it could be their faces locked in a kiss. There could be an ice man who would re-sculpt it when it got droopy. He could live underground. One time, maybe he could show her how to use the chainsaw. She would like that.

The Monkey Handler

After many coy encounters in the Simulator, the tension was taut as a blown balloon. Dale wanted to burst it, stab it, squeeze it. He hadn't called a woman in years. Sexual contact with a crewmember was absolutely forbidden in space, but they were on land for two days. It was a technicality, but to Dale the nights in between seemed wildly open. The first night, he lay in bed dreaming of the second. On the second, he dialed it and waited, clearing his throat after each ring, then tumbling into the void, the unnatural sound of her answering machine. "Holly here!" it began, then continued into a song. No astronaut would ever have that message. It was ridiculous, it was cheesy, he hung up immediately.

She had astronaut's blood, he had to keep reminding himself. Her parents and their hand-in-hand moonwalk, *the space promenade*, printed on posters and tote bags, illustrated on stamps for its ten-year anniversary. Tomorrow would be its 30th. He sat in panicky aftermath of the call. He threw himself in the shower. After, he sat shivering in a worn towel, feeling old. He jumped at the sound of his phone. He rushed to it and saw her name blinking on the screen. Pressing it to his damp ear, he said "Hello Holly!" and waited, goose-bumped, happy. A muffled conversation relayed back, a car horn, swishing. He said "hello" once more, but the muffling kept on. He heard Holly's girlish laugh dazzle some earth place, some usual plaza where everyone's hair was hanging down, everyone's feet touching ground.

Dale was tall and slender with an accusatory nose, sullen, slack cheeks, the same style glasses he'd worn as a boy. Long teeth with prominent gums. Skinny arms with bulging biceps. He sat on the edge of the tub in his humid bathroom, toilet water trembling from a recent flush, and finally accepted that no one had dialed the call. Holly was out with friends, Holly was getting undressed in a hotel, one butt cheek had randomly chosen his name. She was in a taxi, she was young, she had no idea. He dropped his towel in a sad lump on the floor and left the bathroom. She was the sexiest woman he'd ever seen in a spacesuit. If he were patient, he might hear her have sex with a stranger. This disgusted him. He flipped his phone shut and hastily pulled his underwear on. Earlier, he had prepared a sandwich so painstakingly, with a knife for every spread, paper-thin tomato slices, such an array of cheeses that he'd felt embarrassed of the whole ordeal and sulkily had left the sandwich alone on its plate. Now, dashing into the kitchen, the 29th man to dance the moon sank his teeth into that sandwich.

A dismal night was spent at home, but the morning found Dale driving to Base, an astronaut alive. His medical check-up further perked him up and by the time he saw Holly at the traditional breakfast, "Did you call me last night?" "Oh, did I?" there was no discrepancy a muffin couldn't solve, and one crumbled into his mouth like a supportive crowd.

Looking out from the spaceship, Earth filled Holly's field of vision. A great pile-up of smoke marked where the shuttle had launched. Her heart beat in a lagging, longing, sped-up way. She felt fat in her spacesuit, but she'd only have to wear it for launching and landing. It was stupid to feel fat. She was on a spaceship for Christsake! Holly watched Dale, Justine, and Rory carefully monitor all the levers and lights. Even the monkey was wearing a spacesuit! He was buckled into the seat right next to her. This was truly a privilege for her and the monkey handler, onboard with three overqualified crewmates. That was the toast she had made at the breakfast.

The ground curved, the Earth looking finally like a huge globe! Then like a domed stadium. It fell to a size Holly could hold in her arms, a basketball, volleyball, tennis ball, ping pong ball, a marble, an eye. It stayed an eye. Justine motioned to Rory. Rory pulled a lever. Everyone was quiet. It was unwritten code to remain silent during a launch. Anything more than eye contact is bad luck. Holly knew this, she'd been told, she told herself this again. At any moment some doomed level might react, nothing is perfect, no plan immune.

The silence was also like a moment of silence, ritual, like for dead astronauts. Dead astronauts whose souls float about outer space, along with the meteors and whatever else. Holly didn't really believe that, like about souls, but to die in outer space? What a thing to do out there. Soon she would be shitting in outer space, sneezing. If she cried, if she dared, would her tears float, would they splat on Rory's face?

She looked at the Earth eye. Slowly, it shrank to the size of something pulled off a sweater. Holly reached for the hand of the handsome chimpanzee and he held hers back. His name was Costello. She squeezed. He squeezed. Costello's other hand was held by his handler. Together, Holly, the monkey, and the monkey handler were a chain. If they were playing tag and the monkey handler was touching base, then she and the monkey would also be counted as safe, thought Holly. She laughed to herself and Rory gave her a smile, like *soon Holly, soon we can all laugh out loud*.

The cockpit, living quarters and operator's station were located in the forward fuselage. The airlock provided access for spacewalks. The mid-deck contained provisions and storage facilities, sleep stations, lithium hydroxide canisters and other gear, the waste management system, the personal hygiene station. There was an escape capsule for emergencies that could dislodge from the craft. There were exercise machines, a dvd player. There were astronaut journals from old missions. The ceiling, walls, and floor were covered with handles and ropes.

When first built, the *Spec 5* looked sly and modern, but 30 years later, the shiny white had yellowed, scratches and scuffmarks covered its interior, and rust grew on its metal beams. This gave it a homey feel. To Holly, it felt like time-travel, drifting on the very craft her parents manned for their famous launch. Holly was an off-Broadway stage actress, invited to join in a ceremonial mission on the big anniversary. At first, she'd felt nervous around the astronauts, but Rory had been so nice, they got along immediately, and Justine so stoic. Besides, the monkey handler knew far less about space than she, and she was a quick learner.

Dale told her all the names of the astronauts to have reached beyond Low Earth orbit, because his was one. Also, Justine. Justine Boswin became a star astronaut at an early age, and still held the record for youngest woman on the moon. A Time Magazine cover from that time showed her in zero gravity standing very straight, gazing intently at the camera, while behind her, her crewmates were a mass of tangled limbs. Justine was efficient and professional. She moved gracefully about the cabin. She had a crew cut and never referred to her land life.

The crew fell into familiar rhythms. They floated around in their socks. Dale worked on carbon growth experiments while Justine checked all interior and exterior levels, recording endless data. Holly put on Radiohead and Dale scoffed and switched it off. The monkey handler communicated in sign language to his monkey. Holly distracted Rory from her afternoon exercises, making her play theater games. "Say the line again, but this time as the sophisticated old lady." Rory and Holly's laughter distracted Dale and he grimaced. He glowered at the controls. He beamed at space phenomenon. He cleaned the kitchen.

Dale watched miserably as the monkey picked a bit from his nose and then with one finger, casually flicked the bit off, following its tiny path through the air with his big brown eyes, gauging its wayward course. It could go anywhere. It turned and drifted. The monkey lost interest and made a face at Dale. Dale returned with the meanest, ugliest face he could conceive of and Holly saw. Dale's ugliest face was the face of his soul, she thought to herself. She felt hot and tried to breathe herself down. She bumped her way to the Sphere.

One of the few private spaces on the spacecraft was an observational room, a glass Meditation Sphere, where crewmembers were assigned an hour to themselves every day. In the Meditation Sphere, Costello crawled like a spider, Holly practiced flips, and Rory cried. On Earth, Rory never cried. But alone in space with the glaring absence of things, Earth seemed pedestrian, like level one, and this, level two, so complex and refined, absent of all clues and weight. No fluff here, and she could cry for this, how foolish the all of everything seemed in that Sphere, check-out lines and ATM machines, karaoke, bumper stickers, game shows, ties, dresses, all that stuff, attics full of stuff, closets full, dressers full, fortune cookies, aprons, quilts, trophies, pinwheels, nail polish. In space, she was free of these, she was alone and she could cry.

Onboard the *Spec 5*, Dale flirted with Holly to unusually absent results. Differences between the Simulator and real space typically occur, but this difference was felt so keenly that Dale experienced early stages of Space Adaptation Syndrome (SAS), which he had never suffered before. He took vitamins, did exercises, but his eyes were hot on Holly. Holly clumsily washing her hair with water bags. Holly signing to the monkey, dancing with the monkey, playing with magnets and balls of spit. Holly playing Tetris on the computer, reading Isaac Asimov books, Holly happily indulging in every space cliché he'd ever heard of. His nausea grew worse. Holly and the handler should have been getting SAS, most first time space visitors did. Instead, they wafted about, discussing space like two stoned teenagers, while sweaty Dale silently endured his symptoms, fumbling after a pill that floated past him and into the monkey's open hand.

Costello had been commissioned by a publishing company to write a short book about his trip. His handler was doubtful. "Sure, he's smart. But he's not particularly literary. His jokes are mostly physical and won't translate. I'm more his friend than anything else." The monkey handler had lied on his medical exam, neglecting to admit he was a smoker. When asked if Costello smoked, his handler laughed and the nurse laughed too. She hastily checked *no*, but man how many cigarettes they'd split between them! On car rides to deaf schools, in the woods behind Costello's lab habitat. Costello smoked long before he met the handler. Before meeting Costello, the handler had always refused cigarettes, even when he played in jazz clubs (trumpet) where the air was thick with blue smoke. Costello had many qualities to admire, but when he held a lit cigarette in his big hands and ruefully pulled it to his lips, his handler was re-reminded of Costello's infinite attitude and presence. Anything good for Costello was good for him too, so as soon as the deal went through, he and Costello went strictly on the patch.

The monkey handler had guiltily smuggled the patches onboard. Just his luck if the patches didn't agree with the special air in the spacecraft. When asked about the patch on Costello's butt, he said it was a vitamin supplement. Patches helped, but he and Costello both craved cigarettes, making it one of Costello's most frequent signs. When the handler interviewed Costello to generate content for his book, Costello would reply, *Cigarette. I don't know outer space. Cigarette.* His handler tentatively titled the book *I Don't Know Outer Space* and transcribed all of Costello's replies. *There are not trees. Not birds. Not Martha. Hungry. Cigarette please. You my friend. Walking strange.*

Sometimes on the *Spec 5*, Holly reminisced about the Simulator. How she'd spun in the Simo! Euphoric waves rushed her brain. Weightlessness unbound her thoughts and they flashed casual in her head, skipping around, teasing. Any movement was a joke and Dale was laughing with her. The ballet of the everyday! Slowly, the instant joy had dissolved into calmness. Eventually, she was sorry to admit, the calmness carried the gloss of boredom. She held a rope on the wall and watched the same people she'd been watching. Watched them doing nothing. Would space be as boring as this? She wouldn't mind. She probably wouldn't mind. How could she mind? There wasn't a choice. She decided she wouldn't mind. She did a little dance to boost her disposition and Dale laughed. She felt drowsy with relief. She knew once she got up there she'd feel romantic. Boredom and adventure always dragged out romance and this would be so much of both.

Rory was doing routine examination on the *Spec 5* when she realized the computers in the dislodge capsule weren't working. The air control levels and circulator still worked, and the mini waste system, but there was an error in the main computer. Justine ran a built-in diagnostic program. Dale blamed Costello. To him the monkey was a mammoth toddler, sign language or not. "This isn't just some video game," Dale said. He found the monkey and his handler to be messy crewmates. Costello, in particular, was a sloppy eater, and had room for improvement with the space toilet. His toys were always drifting into Dale's lab.

The monkey handler was gullible and easy to be with. His face was untried and new, he looked like a child actor grown older. He knew nothing about space. He'd attempted to explain the scope and importance of the trip to Costello, but was unsuccessful. "He doesn't understand books to begin with, and he's only once been on an airplane, let alone a space shuttle." Dale pitied this monkey handler. "The *Spec 5* is actually an orbiter, a winged spaceplane, the shuttle is the apparatus that blasted us off," Dale explained haughtily. Not everyone deserved space was Dale's theory. Space was elite. It wasn't for the sloppy or foolish, the unambitious or annoying.

Playing catch with Costello and the monkey handler, Holly overthrew the ball into mid-deck. The monkey handler and Holly climbed rope to rope racing after it. Costello leapt about distractedly, drifting into Dale's lab. For once, it was empty, and Costello poked around. He played with a floating pencil tied to a string. He went sniffing every surface, opened a jar containing soil and cathartically jammed his hands in. Eventually, he busied himself snacking on one of many potted plants anchored to the table, arranged neatly in Dale's control group. Its leaves were lazy and familiar. Costello disliked the taste and spit them out. Soggy leaves bobbed in front of his eyes. The jungle! He tore another leaf from a plant. It ripped easily and he ripped another.

Dale was instantly furious. His screaming sent the monkey handler rushing over, apologetic and blushing. Bitten leaves spiraled around them.Costello grinned and frowned, stood smirking and falling into the wall. The monkey handler rushed around cleaning up. After a lengthy groan, Dale commanded the faulty dislodge capsule be converted into Costello's room.

They outfitted it with snacks and a stereo, and when Rory needed a break from her work, she'd tumble into the dislodge capsule where Costello, the monkey handler, and Holly were all making necklaces out of toothpicks and dates or dancing to the same Rolling Stones CD they'd found in the player when they boarded. Rory became friends with Costello. She taught him how to thumb wrestle.

On Earth and in space, humans prove themselves human. Circular thinking, temporary joys. A Hall and Oates song will bring on the same feelings. Waiting for Costello to get out of the bathroom, the monkey handler slowly peddled on the stationary bike. Holly signed him something. Rory saw and absently tried to translate. *I'm hungry happy. This day has time*. Rory couldn't remember the signs Holly had taught her.

The monkey handler met Holly in the Meditation Sphere. Holly was used to the weight of a man. Pushing and leaning, letting down on top of her, her breasts usually rolled and flopped how all do. Her butt was a weight that kept her thoughts from lofting. In space, sex was astounding. They laughed it was so great, maneuvering in one position then spinning spontaneously into others. The monkey handler held the ceiling handles and Holly floated freely. Her breasts were buoyant as floats. Sex made sense in outer space. His penis was a thing that kept them together.

One day, Dale suited up in full gear and to much fanfare ventured in the airlock and out the explore hatch. Hovering in *real-deal space* as Holly called it, he tethered a satellite to the *Spec 5's* exterior. They watched Dale from a porthole and Holly whispered to the monkey handler, "This is like Star Trek!" He smiled and she said, "I mean, more than usual." With a grin, Rory started the craft back in motion with Dale still outside. His startled scream sent Holly hysterical and he admonished them from his headset. Justine couldn't help laughing as she regained control of the spacecraft. When Dale climbed in the airlock, he tried to laugh. Slowly, he unsuited. To Rory's apology he gave a forced smile then disappeared into his lab.

Exiting the Meditation Sphere, Holly tried to smooth her hair, but it had been messy the whole trip. Inside, the monkey handler was still struggling to get dressed. With their clothes flying around, it sometimes reminded him of a washing machine. Holly tried to lean against the wall while fixing her bra. When she looked up, Dale was glaring at her from mid-deck. Her hands went to fix her hair. Her hair was unfixable and she stared back. A bit of fuzz flew through the air, and she instinctually leapt for it, as if it were evidence.

Dale screamed at Holly, but it was hard to hear what. He drifted into the wall and then punched the wall. He propelled himself away from her. He spotted Costello on the ceiling and threw a water bag at him, but it drifted downwards instead. He floated angrily into the kitchen area and squeezed a banana from its peel. Costello tried to catch it. The banana wobbled through the air, peel-less, naked. Dale gave a snort, then squeezed all the bananas from their peels. He threw open the food drawers and tossed out the vitamin pellets, trail mix, the M & Ms, freeze-dried steak, powdered soup, all into the air where they formed a swarm of junk. Rory heard the commotion and walked into the mess. She put her hands in and tried to clear a space. She tried to find a bag, a bin, anything, but Dale was in her way. If she could just herd the mess. Holly pushed her way through and Dale pushed her back. Justine couldn't see past the mess. Dale advanced towards Holly, flailing and wild, he shoved her back into Costello's room. Rory tried to hang onto her, but he shoved her too. Justine tried to calm Costello, who was rushing towards the group, and it happened so quickly, in the thick of hundreds of hovering M&Ms, the trail mix and water bags, vitamins floating in a mass like a convenience store destroyed, the sliding dislodge door shut and locked, and Justine, Holly, Rory and Costello were launched in the faulty capsule while Dale fumed in the *Spec 5*, the monkey handler in the Sphere, still fumbling after his socks.

The four space stragglers drifted through relatively empty regions of the universe. There was dark matter and dark energy. There was *cosmic microwave background radiation*, but Holly had since stopped asking for definitions. She knew there was no friction in space and she felt this now, in a faulty dislodge capsule with two astronauts and an adolescent male chimp. In their possession, the dislodge capsule (a 15' x 10' x 10' interior space complete with the same ropes and handles they'd grown so used to), a space toilet, two sleeping bags (with ties to hold them down), a CD player, a CD, Costello's collection of rubber balls, a plant that died in one of Dale's experiments, pictures of Thelonious Monk, Jane Goodall, and Manny Ramirez that the monkey handler and Costello had taped to the walls days earlier, Costello's hairbrush, an early draft of Costello's *I Don't Know Outer Space*, a deck of space cards (made with Velcro and played on a special board), a stash of nicotine patches and an extensive medical kit. There were water bags and snacks, but only enough for a few days. Justine calculated their daily allotment.

Their initial hours in the capsule were wrought with dread. Holly would cry and the others didn't reassure her, they shared the same cold fate. Costello signed that the monkey handler was his best friend. He signed that he hoped he would see him soon and Holly quickly signed *soon!* Rory and Justine spoke of Dale with pent-up hatred, recalling every prickish thing he'd ever done, said, thought, insinuated. Then they couldn't stand his name and no one would utter it.

The confusion, anger, and panic melted to something jokes could cut through and they tried to enjoy their last hours. "We've already died. To float in space is already death," said Rory. Holly agreed. It was unnatural to be alive so far from their habitat. Holly took Rory's hair out of its bun. She braided it and then undid the braid. "When I was 13 and was just starting to use deodorant, I used to put it behind my knees and on the insides of my elbows. I thought any angle like that you were supposed to put deodorant on." Holly combed the hair with her fingers, she divided it in half. "I used to sneak downstairs in the middle of the night. I was like five years old. I would eat butter like it was a bar of chocolate." Holly had Rory hold one section of hair. She had invented three new kinds of French braid since they'd begun their *final mission*, as Rory called it.

Exile on Main Street was played frequently, and though back on ground Holly would have claimed to know all the words, having listened to that album so much in college, she now saw her prior knowledge was only the meager beginnings of the in-depth relationship that she and *Exile* were fated to share. They were all experts on it and close listenings led them to wonder if *The sunshine bores the daylights out of me/ Chasing shadows moonlight mystery* was a reference to space travel. Were they *chasing shadows moonlight mystery*? Justine said they were barely moving. They were reaching.

Holly taught Rory and Justine all the sign language she knew, and through performance, Costello taught them more. He taught them *cigarette*. He taught them *car, chair, dirt, tree*. They had a jumping jack contest. They got tired. They got antsy. They cried and felt bad for themselves.

Rory did a breathing exercise while Holly closed her eyes and recited her memories. "There was a farm scene painted on my wallpaper, repeated again and again in a pattern. I climbed out of my crib and got two black eyes. I was not hurt, but every time I saw myself in the mirror, I would scream." Rory buckled herself to the wall and did leg stretches. "He was the cutest boy in school and we were the first kids to 'go out,' so all our friends were really excited. Our parents would drop us at the movies and we'd be in this huge group of kids. He kissed my hand on the bus and it was a big deal."

Costello told them about learning sign language, how he always knew how, because his mother was a 'signer,' and so signed to him when he was a baby. Costello had been to many jungles and met many monkeys. He had signed with children all over the world. He did not like working on his book. Holly urged him to finish it, but he refused to talk about space. Holly taught him how to give a massage. They played "Rock Paper Scissor," which always made Costello laugh, and with vigor he bashed the scissor and cut the paper, emphatically he covered the rock. But Costello grew bored and homesick, and the

THE MONKEY HANDLER   81

others felt the same. They slept and dreamt. Holly had a dream where Dale rescued them and they laughed at him. She had one where she was making out with Justine. She didn't share these dreams. Rory had a dream where Costello had a baby and this dream they all liked. Costello thought it was a good idea. When Rory brushed him, he wanted to keep the wad of hair, his *baby*.

Justine found cyanide pills in the medical kit on the wall and took one out. Rory objected, "Don't abandon us on our final mission! Don't you want to feel it?" Justine smiled and caught the ball Costello threw towards her. She said, "I'd like to feel it right now, here, with you two blabbering, not starved, crazed and anxious, my heart beating some ungodly number." But they drew her out. They charmed her. Rory read aloud from *I Don't Know Outer Space. Where is your trumpet? Why? New food? Hungry now. Cigarettes why? Me and Holly danced. My ball is lost. My red one. Cigarette please. You are my friend. Space? I don't know Outer space. I know the trees. I know Martha.*

Justine told them about her husband for the first time. He was an engineer. He was quiet. He was brilliant. When she met him he had a moustache, then he had a beard, now he had nothing. He was good with animals. He made great pancakes. The women wanted a buffet, to wander in a museum, to run down the street. It would be nice to fry some fish, walk a mountain, to get caught in the rain, to run into an acquaintance. A drink, a phone call, to read a newspaper! They wanted to climb trees with Costello. To take a shower, ice skate, to lie on a carpeted floor. *Who is Martha*, Rory asked. Costello did not respond.

Holly had broken astronaut code, and at first that had stilled her. Guilt had spread in full-body regret, but Dale had broken a code too, and space travel was so brash, space travel had broken some code as well. And all codes get broken, that's why people made codes, but outer space didn't have codes, outer space was still and waiting. It was quiet and watching. It was endless and neutral.

Outer space is not completely empty. It contains a low density of cosmic rays, plasma and dust. Different regions are defined by the winds that dominate within them. The *Spec 5* swayed a few miles from the dislodge capsule. Dale had barred the door to the Sphere with the monkey handler stuck inside. The snack swarm had dispersed equally throughout the cabin. It had a queer, festive look. Dale drifted about the craft, eating whatever his hand caught. He watched the monkey handler from a very small window. At first, the monkey handler was interesting to watch. He cried and yelled, he exercised, he sang, he whispered, but then he got weak and listless. He drifted in and out of consciousness.

Dale's breathing was repetitive. His mind, it was stuck. Every now and then there was the thump of the monkey handler's head hitting the glass Sphere. To Dale, it was familiar, like a distant clock, a neighbor's pet. Dale loosely held a rope. His eyes were shut, listening for the thump. He put a hand on his face, he forgot what he was listening for. He opened his mouth absently, then, there it was, there it was again. The sound. The sound reminded him of something he knew, that knew him. The food knew him, but only sometimes it cared. Sometimes he'd eat a bad something, a stale bit among the rest. He'd flinch and wait and not remember for what, and then the thump, distant but audible, and Dale was still and then waiting again.

Occasionally, astronaut crews attempt a reunion. A husband is sent out with the kids. Picking through her stack of CDs, an ex-astronaut decides on Brian Eno, then at the last moment, turns on the radio. Her astronauts arrive abruptly, spreading out on the couch, drinking wine, feeling the rug with their feet. They have all put on weight, except for Gordon, who grins at them from a skeleton head, his shirt hanging on his chest like a flag.

Someone makes a joke and the laughter elevates them. They beam at each other, waiting for the next joke, praying for it, but then silence. They look around the silence and grow used to this as well. They hope no one will make a joke. They wait expectantly and no one does. If they danced, the room would temporarily hold their energy, but no one much feels like it. They lie in the woman's backyard and look at the stars. But the black of the sky is grainy. It always is, on Earth. The air smells too much like grass. Gracefully, one gets up to make an exit and the others follow in unison. It is pleasant to be near each other, but also pleasant to get in separate cars and hear their doors shut, to start their engines, reverse, brake, and drive away in all different directions.

The Sad Girlfriend

She and her analyst spend the nicer part of an afternoon analyzing a "l-o-v-e" stuck on the end of a letter. "Is it hyphenated for emphasis?"

"No, the dashes are sticks in the love. They cut up the word. They spread the love thin across the page. It is a weak love."

"The hyphens are chains?"

"The hyphens are needles."

"What if the hyphens are just playful? Maybe they are influenced by hip hop music."

"They are needles." A sigh escapes from the air-conditioner. "I am confident they are needles."

Wednesdays are beginners' class yoga. She sits in her spot. During a pause, she falls asleep. The others assume she is meditating. They try not to stare. They stretch. The sad girlfriend wakes with a start. She licks the drool on her cheek. "I was just meditating," she explains loudly. The others nod.

"What did you see?" they whisper. "What did you find out?"

A portrait of a sad girlfriend can find shade in many silhouettes. Trying to cry on the toilet. Struggling with the passenger-side seatbelt. Scowling under the weight of an arm. Growing up, girls ambition to be girlfriends. Birthday candles die for it.

"At first it was black. I could hear you calling out downward dog. I saw numbers and the numbers were in colors. Then I was in a Starbucks, except everything was made of water. The floor was shallow water, the walls were deep. There were different cups and each one held inside it a joke." A murmur moves across the class. "What kind of joke?" "Did you try the joke?" "Was I in your meditation?" The yoga teacher silences them with a hand movement.

Tim McWilliams eyes his girlfriend through his glasses. Sad again? And over what? Strawberry ice-cream thrown in with the chocolate and vanilla? Can't a spoon spoon around it? "Strawberry ice cream tastes nothing like strawberries. It is just an unpleasant reminder." Tim

McWilliams has spent a fortune on Blockbuster new releases. Can't the night recover in the dark?

It can seem that nothing is happening. The clouds do their thing over buildings. The commercials cue up at commercial breaks. A story meanders without any discernible plot. But behind these blinds, a world is breathing breaths on top of breaths already breathed. Brad Pitt is slowly falling out of love and into a new love. Matter into energy, energy into light.

The sad girlfriend paints her nails with polish. She decides to change outfits before the polish has time to dry. It smudges. She does not cry. She wipes the smudged nail on toilet paper and the toilet paper sticks. She uses nail polish remover, which gets her high. Or doesn't get her high. Or does get her high. She checks gmail. She checks gmail. She checks gmail.

"A Kim Basinger movie made my relationship look boring." The clock drags its minute hand constant and even.

"What first attracted you to Tim?" The analyst asks, searching her hair for split-ends.

The sad girlfriend waits for the subway pressing her Metrocard to her lips. She walks to the edge of the platform and peers down the tunnel. *Where are the bright eyes of the train*? A couple leans against the wall waiting, hugging out of boredom. The train comes. Everyone sits down. The train pulls out. Inside the car, no one moves. The eyes of the passengers roam uneasily over the advertisements, onto the other passengers, then quickly out the window to the lonely tunnels with their repetitive graffiti tags. "We were in a swimming pool and his eyelashes clung together like tips of a crown. That was attractive to me."

The sad girlfriend feels a feeling in her stomach. She sits very still. There are no other girls in her car. She folds her arms across her boobs. She makes an unattractive face. *There is a big shit in my stomach and it won't come out my butt.* The subway car halts to a stop. The analyst floats into Starbucks, "Why do you think this is?" I think it's scared. The passengers keep their faces straight. If the sad girlfriend lets her eyes linger too long on any one man, the man might later log on to Craigslist and post a missed connections entry.

The sad girlfriend searches for a small child to keep her faith in. During subway halts, she finds it helpful to focus her fear and hope onto a small child. There are none in sight. The lights cut out. The subway car waits in the anxious dark. *Probably, terrorists have killed the subway driver.* The analyst pinches her fingers on the thin half-hairs of the split end. It will either be gas that knocks everyone in comas or they'll come in with knifes, bullets, flames. The terrorists keep going after New York cause it's the big American pinball machine. Its skyline stands like bottles in a row, waiting to be knocked down saloon-style. There is no announcement from the subway conductor. The analyst pulls to see how far up the split end will split. The girlfriend searches again for a child.

In this year of early '00s, anxiety is indoors. It's being surrounded by still objects, walls too white and too smooth. Outside, the trees swish, the birds chatter, an ant will crawl over your leg and include you. But inside the only sound to accompany the air-conditioner is the metallic whine of a miss-programmed wake up alarm. M4w, E train 3 am: You were the sad girl wearing a blue t-shirt and white/light grey shorts. Me, tan khakis, black shirt w/white logo, black glasses, bob marley was playing on my iPod shuffle. You had wavy hair tied back, then you let it down. You have an amazing natural beauty.

The sad girlfriend rubs her Metrocard on her face. The ink has stained her nose. Is it ever worth wearing a dress? In the day it can feel relaxing, but by night it's just a flag waving to the rapists. The sad girlfriend realizes her eyes have been resting in someone else's eyes. The someone else smiles. You sat by the door. I stole a few glances, didn't stare, but totally wanted to. You were breathtaking. If you happen to read this and are available/interested send me a email.

Sometimes landing a boyfriend feels like being drafted in the NBA. *Well, I've always wanted to play, ever since I was little watching games. I think I can really help this ballclub out of its recent difficulties.* Which thought will be the last to sulk around her brain understood? Her family feels as far away as a wallet-sized photograph. Her tombstone will stand straight while Brad Pitt's life continues its wayward path.

Above the subway, the world is living its noisy way.
A.M. eyes are dizzy from Craigslist. Bulky guys flash
little lights over driver's licenses. Why were buildings
built over our sky? It's only occasionally when we see the
moon, but it's supposed to be the main thing up there.
You take the train from Astoria to Manhattan. You're
about 5'6", petite, really cute short dark hair, always dress
casually; tee shirt, cargo pants, etc. I think you're greek.
You never smile. You are so unbelievably sexy and rarely
look up from your sudoku.

The world has already ended. It ended when Chris
Columbus peed on land. When Jesus died and everyone
got obsessed with him. In 2000 when everything was going
to fuck up and then nothing fucked up at all. The whole
next millennium lay open, its ten centuries available, its
decades in rows. No one is watching us lay toilet paper
on wet public toilet seats. We carry our water in cups,
draw sunglasses on our sun. I should've said something
but couldn't think of anything unlame to say. You looked
so tired, slouching in your tank top. Let me take care of
you. I see you most every working day. We enter the train
thru the same set of doors and exit at Penn. You have dark
shoulder length hair, which is sometimes still wet in the
morning. I am too shy to say hi. I was amazed by your
beauty and was in awe and I am never in awe of anyone
or anything. Eventually I'll have to say something to you,
maybe when I see you walking down 22nd to the stop,
flip-flops pattering out the beats of my heart. You sat with
me until i got off at times sq. the conductor said be careful

to the 59th st. stop and i said careful of what? we looked at each other and you similed.

The girlfriend may die a terrible death of terrorists. There will be no children to watch with honest eyes. The analyst will be so upset. The sad girlfriend had tried to watch the world news, but the stories lacked the details needed to engage her. Brad Pitt fell for a girl who doesn't wear shoes when she doesn't want to. To have a boyfriend is to play in the privileged center of a story. To be sad is to hang low, matching mind to gravity, to feel the indoors and outdoors so hard it makes your head ring. This is being written to the angel who shared her bottle of water with a homeless person during the heat wave. You were wearing a beige see-through outfit. You had a beautiful golden complexion. I believe you are Italian. I hope that you are out there.

Infections

William sat by the dry reflecting pool and ate his bagel without Justin. Here they would sit on a Sunday, after a long night of blowjobs and iTunes. William poked extra cream cheese out the bagel's hole, letting it fall to the concrete. Like all city parks, Rittenhouse Square idealizes the nature everyone is missing out on, William would say to Justin. It's a biblical fantasy. Parks make trees a fetish thing. But Justin's thoughts would be lost in the refection pool, then full, approving how his eyes and nose and mouth made aesthetic sense together, while the faces of other park-goers seemed genetically slapped together, mutated into adult finality.

In Anatomy, William and his group were given a dead body. The hardest part to saw apart was the teeth. William let the girls do that part. It was an old woman's body and having never seen one in real life, he was unprepared for the intricacy of a vagina. The skin is divided into folds, lying between the legs like a lizard in the sun, William wrote in his notebook. It feels as though the lizard hasn't moved in hours, but might at any second slowly shift its weight. William nudged closer for a better look. He pushed his rubber-gloved finger against the vagina. The other boy in the group raised his eyebrows at William, implying. William informed him that he was gay. The boy looked at him. William said something in a gay-sounding voice that made the girls smile. Then the boy moved closer to William and the vagina. "Well, usually this part is way more pink, and it's sort of wet over here, like with an oil or shine or something." The girls squirmed as he described this.

At Woody's, the dance floor was crowded with muscle-flexers, as usual. William danced near a cute boy with glasses. An older unattractive man danced towards William. In a series of moves, William escaped from the unattractive man. He danced up to the cute boy with glasses, but the cute boy danced into the center of the floor. William's dancing slowed as muscle-flexers filled the spot abandoned by the cute boy.

Drunk leaving Woody's, he tripped on the pavement. Blood ran up to the surface of his scraped knees. William knew that in humans, oxygenated blood was bright red. He knew that deoxygenated blood was a darker shade of red. Also, there was a rare condition, sulfhemoglobinemia, that resulted in green blood, blah blah blah. He knew all about it. He looked at the blood on his knee and felt privileged to have his body. He didn't bother cleaning the dirt from the cuts.

Justin's homeless friend was sleeping in the doorway when William wandered back to his apartment. William looked with interest at the man's slender arms. If the man were dead like in Anatomy, then William could touch the man's arm. The man woke and looked at him, "Justin home?" he said. William wiped at his bleeding knees.

"Justin has left his home forever."

"Shame." The man put his fingers to his eyes, "He leave his anti-anxieties?"

"I don't know. I didn't check. Maybe. I don't know."

"He'd been giving me his anti-anxieties. Made him too dizzy." William considered the man. If he were the man, he would get more tattoos. Sometimes, one looked lonely alone on an arm. William looked at a scratch on the man's knuckle. "Hey, that looks kind of infected."

"That so? You tell me, Medicine Man." William smirked and went inside.

In the bathroom, he brushed his teeth with his new natural toothpaste. As he sat on the toilet, he stared at the stupid inspirational poster Justin had left behind. *Learn to watch snails. Plant impossible gardens Make little signs that say Yes! and post them all over your walls.* Yeah Right. William stayed up late looking at his diseases textbook, skimming for the strange and unusual. Black hairy tongue was a harmless condition sometimes caused by Pepto-Bismol.

William found himself on the website where he met Justin. Justin's profile still read the same. "I used to be religious. Turns out I just like mythology." William reread the whole thing, idly highlighting with the cursor. "My hair often has its own ideas about how it wants to be styled." Some sentences in the profile rang false, "I often have dark circles under my eyes because I love to sleep." Also, "I am a cross between Angelina Jolie and young Robert De Niro." Yeah Right. Then he highlighted what he hated, "You could spend a lifetime with me and never get to know every facet of my personality, though you'd have a great time trying." That was not true. William highlighted the whole thing blue, then unhighlighted. He considered starting up a fake profile and using it to flirt with Justin. Only if things got boring. Or stressful. If things got so boring or stressful that William felt suicidal, then he would instead start up this fake profile. As a gift to himself. And maybe also if he got slightly suicidal, he might let Justin's cute homeless friend live with him, because the apartment was so big and lonely, plus it would be a good deed!

It was the semester when William and his classmates were paired with different doctors. So far he'd had the dermatologist and the pediatrician. Tomorrow was the oncologist. William searched the medicine cabinet looking for Justin's medicine and found bottles and bottles of it. He gave some to Justin's homeless friend and took some himself when he missed Justin. Which was most times. He stared at his desktop background. He checked his knee and saw no infection. In some ways, it was a shame. Once he had a staph infection and it was not an entirely bad experience. He scrolled down his iTunes library, giving random ratings to each song. When he came to his cousin's album, he gave each song only one star, just to be mean.

On the day of the oncologist, William felt light-headed, but it was just the anti-anxieties. The oncologist poured coffee for him and William, "It's good to make your patients wait a little, makes them respect your time." The oncologist talked as they walked to the first patient of the day. "Ms. Kespetrova's situation is complicated by a breast implant procedure 10 years prior to the cancer." They strolled down the hall side-by-side. "She has an accent." William kept up the pace. "She's a real trip." The oncologist sighed, fingering the cool metal part of his stethoscope. "This is just for show," he joked to William as they walked inside the room. Ms. Kespetrova sat in a fur coat on the examination table.

"I go half crazy in these rooms waiting. Sometimes I go all the way crazy!" She smiled at William. "That is what a doctor should look like!" She nodded approvingly at William. The doctor spoke to William about the left side tumor, showing the most recent ultrasounds.

"I'm just a student," William explained and introduced himself. "I'm sorry to hear of your condition," he continued politely. The Russian woman laughed. "Do not be sorry!" The doctor looked uncomfortable. Ms. Kespetrova screamed, "I get to have it all!" She tugged her fur coat emphatically, "First no breasts, flat chest like a boy, then little tiny ones, then bigger and bigger, healthy full breasts, then bigger breasts for breastfeeding," she sighed, "then tired breasts, swollen nipples, sagging, then surgery and implants and bouncing breasts, and now lump, machines, x-rays. So much attention on my perfect breast and its imperfection, this one," she took off her fur coat and was topless. She shook her large left breast at William, "Soon this breast will be cut away. It will be trash in the bottom of a can. My chest will be lopsided, one-sided, original. My body is always changing." The doctor checked something in his cell phone. Ms. Kespetrova continued, "Aging does not necessarily have to be a disappointment. I had beautiful grey hair young. It made all the girls want to go and dye it like that. A girlfriend of mine, she had a humongous wedding ring. Diamond the size of a dinner mint. She was walking in Miami Beach late at night, a man on the street cut off her finger. At first, pain and despair, but now everyone admires her for it. She gave something up." William nodded encouragingly. The doctor shook his head. His eyes narrowed on a clump of dust on the floor. "We must be going now, Ms. Kespetrova. Dr. Muller will be in shortly." The doctor motioned to William and they went back into the hall.

"My wife wants me to pick up the kids, but there is no way I'll be out of here in time. The kids are at day care," the doctor said to William. "I need her to pick up the kids, or at least call the other parents to see if they will drive theirs and ours. I, in no way, have time to call the other parents."

Staring at the poster, William tried to think of a cool way to ask the homeless man to move in. He didn't want it to seem like a come on, but why would it seem like a come on? He smiled when he remembered the Russian woman. He knew just what she meant. Sometimes being sick is interesting. *Cry during movies. Cultivate moods.* He was going to have to destroy the poster. What had he been thinking before? The homeless man. Justin? Something about the woman. Like when he had his staph infection, it was so gross and painful and horrifying at first. But then he got used to it and on medication, the pain lessened. He was no longer afraid of the infection. He was intrigued. His body had made something that needed him. He had to change its band-aid each night and check its progress. He had to care for it. Gently, he'd press the infection to ooze out pus. He liked thinking the pus was cum. Also, blood would come out, not dripping out, but in little balls. Balls of blood. Balls of cum. His body had made him something.

The class had to write essays about the week with the different doctors. William's was titled "The Illness as Interesting Life Experience" and was returned to him with a failing grade. "Wha-at?" William asked the paper. His classmates were packing up their books. He ducked out of the classroom. He looked to see his thesis circled and question marked. 'In addition to sympathizing with the patient, the doctor can also treat the illness as an experience, as a creative capability of the body.' William rolled his eyes to himself. God, the medical world is so closed-minded. He started running instead of walking, crossing over to Center City in a hurry, sneaking onto 24th street while the hand sign was blinking red. They're taking the body, a strange, unpredictable, wonderful mess, and they're boiling it down to a syllabus! William breathed in some car exhaust. He stared at the mutant woman on Market Street, her wig plastered to her head, her make-up like a voodoo mask stuck on from last year. Luckily, life can't be contained in a stupid fucking syllabus.

The homeless man cleaned up so nice, just as William had suspected. It was fun to show him the apartment. "This is Justin's mother's couch, but it's mine now. It's ours," he said to include the homeless man. "It's yours," he said to be generous. "It pulls out." Together, they pulled out the bed. It was nice to come home and find the man deep in reading the cookbook and the anatomy book. By now, he claimed to have memorized the anatomy book.

Class was all review for final exams. William leaned back in his chair. Looking at the boys' bodies, he pretended they were corpses and he was to dissect them and re-sect them to form the perfect man. That was the Final Exam. Then he would put the creature back to life like in Rocky Horror and have to blow the creation to get an A. If the penis hadn't been correctly re-attached then an erection would be impossible. It would have Anthony's hair, Jake's full lips, Phil's arms, and Jennifer's eyes, if that were allowed, if he could take one thing from her. Maybe her eyes would mix everything up. The teacher scrawled study questions on the board. William had once heard someone describe a coma as the best rest of her life. Sign me up, he said to himself.

Once, after his wisdom teeth had been taken out, William had taken OxyContin and briefly gone into daydreams. The dreams were convincing. They'd have him in a scene with someone he knew and then someone would tell a joke or share an idea or nothing, then suddenly switch to a new scene. That was how William wanted to live life anyway, a little bit of this, a little bit of something totally different. He didn't want to be one person the whole time.

Sitting cozily in their living room, the homeless man quizzed William for the exam. William could only recall 3 of the 11 facial nerves. He thought that lumber puncture was when the spinal canal narrows and compresses the spinal cord, but that was spinal stenosis, said the homeless man. William didn't remember anything about the medial branches of the posterior divisions of the upper six thoracic nerves. "I haven't been having an easy time studying. The internet is soo distracting." He mixed up mentencephalon and myelencephalon. Whenever he heard pancreas he thought about pancakes. "I've been dizzy. Studying makes me dizzy." William took a cigarette from the man's pack and got up. He took a piss in the bathroom, *cultivate moods*, ripped down the poster, and went back to the living room.

"Your turn," he took the anatomy book and quizzed the homeless man. The endocrine system was communication within the body using hormones made by the hypothalamus, pituary, pineal body, thyroid, parathyroids, and adrenal glands. A sacrum consisted of five bones that were separate at birth, but later fused together into a solid structure. William wiped some sweat from his neck and smelled his hand. "Are you looking at the answer sheet over there?" William looked for a lighter.

"Answer sheet? This is my job application," he flashed the answer sheet at William. William looked up from his cigarette. He could see the homeless man looking flattering in slim-fit scrubs. The homeless man starring in *Grey's Anatomy*. He could see the 'Homeless to Famous' story being churned out of newspaper-making machines.

The homeless man scored William some painkillers like he'd wanted. He stood in William's doorway and tossed William the bottle. He scratched one arm with the other arm. One of these days, William was going to lend him money to get another tattoo. The three-legged dog would look great with something completely different underneath it. Like a name with a date or something.

William signed onto the dating website as his fake name, Skyler. A boy had sent him a message. Bored, William scrolleddown the boy's profile. His pictures showed him drunk on two different holidays, then once playing devil sticks in his living room. William took one of the Percocets, then went back to the computer. He looked at profiles, "I was a computer science major at Temple, although I think I'm ultimately going to become a shaman of some sort," but then his eyes didn't want to do that anymore. He pushed his burning Powerbook from his lap. Running windows on a Mac made him love the anonymity of windows. The gay dating site wasn't up to par. Like it left this aftertaste of disgust. Was that how dating sites worked? Was there a way around that?

William felt for his cell phone because there was a noise it had to make. For tomorrow, if he was going to wake for the exam, then there was an important noise for the phone. A girl stuck her gum to a sign post and then walked down the street. William watched and realized she was part of the drug. In a car, it was him and the homeless guy. The trees passed. The street passed. Totally random. William was happy the drug was good at being a drug. Like what if the drug was only good at looking good in a bottle? Justin sat down, "You see I got this haircut, but it's making me hate myself." "I don't want you to hate yourself," William said, giggling. For some reason computers always asked if they should save files, when the files hadn't even been changed. It was a nervous habit of computers.

William sat with his uncle in a church. "I wanted to see a bunch of little scenes. I wanted life to move fast, but I think it's moving slow." His uncle nodded and said, "I mean that's why I moved away. It wasn't a right fit. Everyone looked at me strange because I was tall." William waited in line in a restaurant, "I thought it would be scenes." Wind blew each leaf on a tree. The clouds looked nothing like animals. The drug was making scenes. His "Illness as Interesting" paper had made sense in the computer. All the letters were straight next to other letters. There was a lot to celebrate about having a body. Justin said, "Now we can talk about Skyler." William said, "Who?" William's Dad said, "Who?" In the dark, it was obvious again that William would not transform into a doctor, "That's alright, guys. We don't have to talk about me. We should talk about something important. We should talk about the election."

If the blood, for instance, got mixed up with some dirt, then the body would start a war with the dirt, forming a pus wall to block the virus. The virus wants to live and then there's this conflict taking place within the body. William imagined an infection as a fly stuck in an egg yolk, as a bad smell traveling through a car window. A thing clinging on that didn't belong. Justin infecting the New York gay/queer/trans social scene. William infecting UPenn Med School.

The body can start sending out bad messages. The body can make things you don't want it to make. The paper must've been in the completely utterly totally incorrect font. Many eyes wouldn't have been able to comprehend the font, maybe. Possibly, it was just a wrong font.

Then it changed back to William and the homeless man in the car. The homeless man drove quickly wavering in and out of the lines. From the passenger seat, William looked out his window, then at the beautiful face of the homeless man. The homeless man was swerving. His eyes looked like he hadn't gone to sleep for most of his life. The homeless man turned and said, "If you want me to drive, I could just drive instead." William didn't understand. The homeless man drove on, gripping the wheel. He missed another line. He looked at William and said, "Man, your eyes look like you bought them used." The car drove half on the grass. A stick got stuck in the tire, then snapped. The homeless man looked at William, "You don't have to drive the whole way. I know you, you get tired."

My Boyfriend, but Tragic

I called him Peek-a-boo Street, love bug, baby, Tom Tom Club, Tomato, boy toy, butt man, robo-butt. Our favorite way was to have sex. He was a good cook but serious. His deodorant made me woozy.

This love was my favorite. My other boyfriends had been before. This love was now and it leaked all over. Like since I was in love, so was my apartment. The toilet brush bristled with inspiration! I threw it out because it smelled bad.

This love was big and swallowed reality. I'm not saying the love was merely symbolic. Just the emotions were so massive and bulky, everything else became off-hand. The love wasn't a big deal. It was love. Like a kiss, it's distracting. I worked at a store. Tom worked in a place. We lived smack in the middle of everything. Then we moved a little out of the way. These are just details. Tom was my favorite person I had ever met. My girlfriends, they were characters stuck in a phone. They were electronic people I could chat with, but they were not as real as Tom. My life with him was on a charmed track, a toy set kept going round and round and so we smiled.

But then Tom 9-11ed.

I don't know how to explain this. It's crazy. What are the odds. I'm still weird about it.

If a love is really good, it gets tragic. God is romantic to a fault. Like a bird is beautiful and then it's killed. I'm not saying it's romantic, it makes you shudder. Staring into the bird, mini-revelations glaze over you, this life with all its visual beauty. You are an innocent. You are bad news. Nothing really matters, you kick the dead bird with your sneaker, no one gets mad, god doesn't care, he was there when the bird died, or he missed it, it doesn't matter. The winter is strained and uncomfortable. The sun burns my skin. It's challenging. Tough love, like your boyfriend holding you down a bit pretending and you both get so turned on you can't stand it, you need to mash his thing all the way into yours. Like if there was a bubble and a butter knife, we'd pierce the bubble with the knife. Its Freudish. If there were a pizza and scissors, we might cut the pizza in long strips. We could cut the pizza into shapes and eat them. But Tom is all done.

He 9-11ed. It hit his upper body and he tumbled. He was in a plane and felt queasy. He stood tall next to his twin and they both caught on fire.

I was inconsolable. My country hurt. It was irritated, but not too bad. I checked my underwear and was unsure. I paid someone to look at it and apparently it was ok. Tom was dead. He was demolished. There were little bits of him, but they were sharp. They were asbestos. My country bonded together. It got racist. It itched and was tested. It wrinkled. It protested.

After Tom, Tom looked like Body Worlds. His arm was an omelet. He looked like an alien. Like throw-up. Like sculpture. He was innovative, avant garde. He was pixeled and low quality.

I do the eating thing, the sleeping thing, but what am I but a crying machine, humming along. Breathing, sighing, waiting. I am an admirer of things, a secret brain of events. Before, I was a responder, a pretty shape, contagious laughing. Now, I am just an animal that can move. An example of a person.

I just want to say it once. Tom was born. He was nice. His parents were nice. He made friends laugh. He sneezed. He wasn't a dancer, but he did dance. Then, Tom joined the big club of done lives. He does not linger around. All of Tom was in a brain. The heart is just a power plant. The spirit, a tissue you crumple.

Tom was trying to newscast, but it got too smoky. He was commemorated on a plate, but the kind you can't eat off of. Tom got mushed in a sandwich. He was bankrupt of parts. He was on clearance, then closed. An airplane missed its mother. Someone ordered clam chowder optimistically. Birds had anxiety attacks. A building got embarrassed.

Tom made my calendar cry. He prayed but it felt funny. It was his body, it wasn't his fault.

Doodle Face

Maybe in high school it seemed cool to get your girlfriend pregnant, raise up babies while you were still babies, lean your tiny new person against a peavey amp while you practiced guitar. By college, we knew it was stupid. We stopped picking out names like "Hella" and "Marmaduke." We realized being young was the only thing we had, so it would be crazy to go and create something younger.

I was hanging with the Daz and we'd lifted a little at the gas station store, just for fun. I did it just to make him laugh. I pocketed a "sexual enhancer," which was a spray that made your dick feel less so you could fuck more. Once we got on the street, I showed him and he laughed and dared me to spray it on my hand, so I sprayed it on his hand. He sprayed it on my face, then his face. We punched each other as hard as we could, which wasn't that hard, but the shit worked, we couldn't feel anything but numb.

Walking across the highway, the cars were inches from our shorts. This kind of glory walk always made me feel like I had just died but nothing had actually happened, that the rules, if there were any, were not going to get me. This feeling was really misleading. All that while, somewhere deep inside a pussy, a sexy place was turning to a health-class place. My sperm had grown some doodly human face. Her egg, smaller than eyes could see, had stretched and puffed and was going to bulge into a whole wrinkly person. When I got my sexy ass into bed, time no longer clicked off. All during the night, the doodly human grew.

The Daz was the only one being real about it. "It's about time someone had Junior," Theo drawled and the jokes came too easy. Everyone wanted to babysit it. Muffy had already bought it baby adidas sneakers. A lot of people said it sucked, but I could see they were still excited. They remembered the high school dream-nightmare and would now live it out through doodle face.

Twenty-three is a sweet-ass age. College is over and yeah that feels a little sandy and low, but there are still huge mouthfuls of time before getting old, before getting famous. Life is unfucked by consequence. You always know it can happen, waking up every morning to a pointy fact, the dread slacking your muscles like strings.

I thought mine would be murder by mistake. Like I'd be driving with Daz in the middle of nowhere, some kid roller skating up ahead, I look over to skip the spoken word on the Outkast CD, and hit the kid dead. What if the next morning and every one after, the kid wakes me by putting pennies on my eyes. Like the kid is in pale colors. Ghosts is what I mean.

There is a way out of everything. In monopoly jail, you can always roll for doubles; you don't always have to pay. I sat with her twice, her name on the written-out list. I poked her with the pencils. I whispered jokes I made up on the spot. I tried to give her head in the bathroom. Anything to relax psycho princess, which is what Daz called her to her face. Psycho princess would not be relaxed. The head made her cry. The jokes made her smirk. When her name was blandly called, she got up ran back down the stairs, breathing out in the street again. Standing in the parking lot. The first time she did it she laughed and I laughed too, but it was cause I had nothing else to do and cause it felt like a huge mass of steel and other metals had fallen in my stomach and there was no human way possible to ever lift it out again. The second time I slapped her across the face.

Daz had been coaching me through it all, preaching to me Buddhist things to relax me, buying me beers, talking me up. His big plan was to take me to this mountain up north where his guru was and show me real live monks.

We were going to wake up and chant with everyone and then meditate, meditate while walking, then through eating, through dishwashing, and so on. I don't know how to meditate, but he said it didn't matter. Then he met this girl and got crazy about her. He says having sex with her is like a shroom trip without the shrooms. He says he's got call waiting.

I got so down last week I didn't just want doodle head dead, but Gina dead and me too, and both our sets of parents dead so they wouldn't have to deal, and then I started rooting for the earth microwaving itself like popcorn, the peace in the middle east war spilling into the Africa wars, sweeping the whole globe in a killing party, murdering off everyone so I wouldn't miss out on anything. Then I listened to Paul Simon a little and that calmed me down a little and I could look at everything from further back. I thought how many sexy places there were for my dick to slip in. All the stoops that were waiting to be smoked on, the movies being made to be criticized, and all the countries that had never caught a glimpse of me and the Daz, catching a glimpse of us and smiling, letting us into their new wet places, rolling us foreign magic cigarettes.

Right before all this shit, I was thinking about breaking it up. It had reached that soggy girlfriend point where it wasn't all that exciting and my own life was starting to grandly separate itself out like milk. Or like cream. The only kind that got me crazy was sex in her butt and part of that was how I was conflicted about it, and another part was she didn't want to. I had both of us convinced it was the only way that felt good for me anymore, that I had done it the other way a million times over and now I had graduated to the next level, something harder, weirder. I got addicted to the horrified feeling it gave me while I did it. What the fuck are you doing? One of my voices would ask another. I don't fucking know, was the response, shown in my wild face and her body jerking forward.

This whole time I've been on the toilet in Penn Station. My shit was all jumpy and I felt like I might puke. Now I don't want to leave. There is no one at my parents' house where I'm going and Daz hasn't texted me back. I haven't talked to my parents' since this happened. I said happy Father's Day in an email. There is a guy in the stall next to me that's been here just as long. Maybe we could both just stay here.

New York is glam and grit. Neon signs, dry lumps of dog shit. I have my head phones on, but I've almost used up my Stones CD. It's my 4th time around and I'm beginning to believe them less. Are they working with me or against me? I duck into Borders and pretend I'm looking for something. 5 minutes left the borders people say. Fuck Borders I say very quiet with the Stones backing me up. I sneak over to literature and read all the

Hemingway last lines. Then I'm back on the street again. Glam and grit, neon shit.

Maybe I'm making this too complicated. Doesn't life start just sleeping, eating and faces? Bobbling around big-headed. I've seen babies. They are brilliant in the bathtub, they make games with the sponges. They make you count while they go under, then surface breathless a second later. It gives you a little high. But then it gets tired. It keeps going and going. You go to sleep and they're alive. You wake up they're alive. Even later when you die, they're still alive.

Gina calls and I kill the call with a button. She calls again and I kill that too. My parents' house has no one home. Fat Gina is what my cell phone calls her, but it's cause this kid is going to be sitting in pale colors at the foot of my bed. Ghosting me. And Fat Gina won't disappear so easy either. These will be the bad gods that hang overhead. If only I had left psycho princess on her own, she'd be pouring all her female mania into a conceptual sculpture. Dogs can be babies, cats can be babies. You don't have to actually have one.

There was a terrible silence in the room. I opened and closed the refrigerator just to make noise. If only the air conditioner would start with its little kick. If the Daz can trip without shrooms, then I can do it without pussy too. I turned on the ceiling fan as a start. I opened all the windows, turned up all the heat. Put on the oldest record

I could find. Filled up the bath tub. Jerked off into the toilet. I drank a beer. It felt a little different.

I don't put on my seatbelt anymore cause I'm hoping I might get hurt. There was a boy in the house and he was sexy as hell, but it didn't matter this night. This night no one cared. It's crazy Daz is in NYC and not texting me back. Even if he's got pussy coming out his mouth and nose and ears. There could be a gay porn called ear, nose, and throat man. Different guys could come in his mouth and ears and nose, and he could be dressed like a doctor. No, like a superhero. The air conditioner kicked on and it felt all of a sudden that things could work out. Long live doodle face. My mom called and I threw my flip phone against the wall. Walked over, picked it up and it was off, but when I turned it back on it seemed fine.

The boy that was sexy as hell was trying to find a way to leave his baby-filled girlfriend without being arrested by the karma police. Ha. Like maybe I'm just in a private funk of catastrophic proportions. Poor little doodle will be born and I'll give him my parents' money and then find some foreign-born girl that's both simple and sophisticated, both, and do it in her ass until I get old.

Hopefully I'll get old gracefully, give up trying to look cool and act cool and feel young and all that, cause that's what it's like when you listen to the Stones 10 times in a row. The songs just happen, the songs lose their minds. Poor little doodle. It's fun to figure things out at first and go places and play the games, and then friends, yeah, it's cool, but there are these long moments, single hours where you end up with these people you are supposed to have fun with, except you don't, you just sit around and get self-conscious. And everyday there is clothing and bathing and dishes and you have to keep saying, "Well this is different this time because," or "I like doing these simple things cause." And that's a problem too. You can convince yourself of anything, convince yourself you like a chick, or don't like her, that the color of your walls puts you on edge, or that those trees outside make you painfully nostalgic. And you're like, cool, maybe I'm an outdoorsy sort of guy, maybe that's why, but then once you're out in the wild, you miss your cell phone like crazy, you miss dance music, microwave popcorn, stupid ass shit. I know I'm going on forever. But I'm sexy as hell and I'll fuck you in my parents' bed if you show up at my door. I'm so sick of myself. If the bath had been warmer, the shroom trip would have worked better, but the water was lukewarm so it didn't feel anything like drugs. It felt like there was a puddle so big I could fit my whole body in its cold dirty center.

Maybe in high school it seemed like a cool idea to fuck your girlfriend pregnant. You'd just rest your crying little girl up against the peavey amp and riff out a lullaby. You'd be like Kurt Cobain, except alive and well. With no bullet in the brain. With no end to the story. But to bring baby into this world is to start part two of your two-part life.

He had a pimple on his back that he couldn't reach with either hand. He opened the medicine cabinet and looked for another mirror, so he could do the thing where you look into the mirror with the other mirror. He couldn't find another mirror. The other day, where was he, he had had two mirrors and that's when he had seen the pimple. He got out a CD and tried to use that. It was too rainbowy. Fuck the pimple. He wanted to tweeze his eyebrows, but resisted. He did a line of coke cause he found some in his parents' bathroom. The air conditioner kicked itself off and don't die he thought, as the sound faded far away.

The beer made his body feel like not moving, and he not moved on his bed. The coke made him feel clear, but then more beer fuzzed him out. The cell phone sat unflipped on his stomach and together he and the phone waited for the nonsense sound of a text message. Sometimes he heard that sound like a ghost in the night, but it wasn't the text message, just a ghost. He texted to the Daz "save me" but the Daz was out, busy, bouncing basketballs against car windows, tripping on drugs with no drugs.

He found he could make tears in his eyes, and they fell warm on his face just like tears, but they couldn't be tears cause he hadn't cried since he was a kid, and now he was some monster almost father, but they felt warm and tear-like they sat on his cheeks feeling sorry for him, each drop a little bit of sorry, each tear a little thing lacking the complexity to be a creature, the power to be alive, but doing more than a drop of water does when spilled from a Poland Spring bottle, not manufactured and handled, but made by his own eyes, a magic way to have his cheeks touched without any person to touch his cheeks.

McGrady's Sweetheart

She was bleeding, but got into bed. He pushed the extra pillows to their feet. The newspaper drifted to the floor. The futon sat on top of a massive rug they'd gotten at a tag sale. They felt a cold thing under the sheets and it was a nickel.

I don't have a tampon and I don't care, she said, if you don't care. She laughed and made a face. He put his hands on her shoulders. Bleed on these sheets, he said, you have fought so gallantly in the war. She shook off his hands. I'm not *that* gallant, she said, I ran from the enemy and tripped on a rock. Bullshit, he said, I heard the shot. He tried to tear the sheet with his teeth. Until the nurses come, he said, I'll stay by. No, she shook her head, run while you still can, the enemy will be crowding the horizon any second. He looked out and the horizon was clear. The ground was all torn up from soldiers' boots. The moon was behind a big fancy piece of cloud. I could never leave you bleeding, McGrady, thinking things that might be the last things you ever think.

What are you thinking now?

While you were in the trench with the boys, I was running free in the wide open. I thought, couldn't we find another excuse? Sure I like my soldier's outfit. What kid doesn't dream up a uniform, real obstacle courses, of being scared? We need a war to sleep outside?

Wallace couldn't stop the bleeding. He sat his back against a giant tree. His helmet had rolled off to some rocks. McGrady sprawled in his lap like an old mutt dog, and heavier. Wallace had lost track of their troop and his radio was acting up. He fiddled with the dial, got some music to calm McGrady, who was still talking last words. Of which there were *a lot*. At first he tried to remember them to tell McGrady's sweetheart and family, but McGrady had lost so much blood as to now lose sense. Wallace held the soldier's soft hands and gazed around at the wilderness, the grass's lazy way of resting on other grass.

McGrady murmured at him, something about animals, how animals sleep as well. McGrady whispered, Blue fields have a say. Wallace decided to agree. I might want to go into tent design, McGrady confessed, maybe after the war. Wallace said tents were a growing field and inquired about potential designs, but McGrady clammed up, blood soaking the grey uniform, dripping into the dirt.

A lunacy permeated the scene. Flies fluttered about screaming. Leaves rustled in eerie agreement. Wallace chewed the same old gum he'd started the day with. His moustache tickled and he sneezed. He listened to the crickets' chant, their limbs whirring incessant and enthused. He saw the sun had sunk low in the horizon, had had the sense to.

A mosquito landed on Wallace's arm and his arm was around McGrady. They watched the mosquito position itself to draw blood. McGrady slapped it and killed it, slipping back unconscious. McGrady's light eyes now shut, Wallace took another look on McGrady's face. Rosy cheeks and a prominent, upturned nose that looked noble and snubbing, sandy, curly hair careless and stuck to a forehead cool with sweat, a switchblade scar on the chin; McGrady looked like some choir kid gone jazz. Wallace expected zonked-out soldiers to look serene, but McGrady's lips were in a sneer. With fingers flaking of dried blood, Wallace nudged McGrady's lips to make a more angelic mouth.

McGrady had shot the best, then Culler, quietly great, unconsciously great, then Lodi, for sheer persistence, almost by mistake Lodi as third, next Horowitz, then the rest all about the same, Wallace, Rogers, Serg. Van Creerie,

Fitsky, Myles. Wallace had met McGrady at training. Watched as the soldier hopped the fence during morning sprints, and rolled a cigarette, tossing a dandelion in with the tobacco. He'd seen then McGrady had style, and admired that. With the only scissors in the Battery, Sergeant Van Creerie had done the boys all trim except for McGrady, who'd refused, walking around with a hairdo. Also the Mess Hall, McGrady could dance. *Really really dance.*

When they all shared pictures of their sweethearts, McGrady wouldn't, said it was private. They could only imagine McGrady's then, and Lodi said it must be a homely one, a nose that looked like ears, an eye with something swimming in there, a face victim, like the men in the ward. Wallace thought the opposite though, a sweetheart too beautiful to share, a cool, knowing nose, eyes that had depth, lips that looked nice. A figure that flattered clothing. A voice that glorified talking. If Wallace concentrated on it, he could conjure that voice, bold and melodic. It was best never to get the name of another soldier's sweetheart, the lying awake time was too wild, took a man's reality and twisted like an ankle.

They hadn't been the slightest prepared. Horowitz was half-shaved when he saw something reflected in his bit of mirror. A bullet whizzed by, and with soap on his face, Horowitz dove into the brush and curled into a ball. He pretended he was dead. He listened to the skirmish, Lodi's cursing, insane laughter. With his eyes hard shut, it was a radio drama. He imagined he was with his sweetheart at the theater. An animal, rabbit maybe, ran flat into his side, but took no lingering moments with Horowitz, immediately scooted off.

After the enemy had up and quit, Horowitz heard the distant sounds of his troop reforming, yet chose to crawl the other direction. He kept low to the ground, dragging his feet through flowers and mud, a broken bottle, pausing at what looked like long johns, weeds, moss, miles of poison ivy, an ant hill of angry red ants, until finally he felt brave enough to stand. He stood, thought of Jeannie once more and limped off. His leg was not injured in any physical sense, but he thought to limp, a sudden blooming of alibi. After a few steps, the limp felt real. He ached for Jeannie, hot legs, funny ways, plus a fear about leaving the boys; it all got solid like gunk in his leg. He limped on. His politics were weak to start with. His honor strong, but on a break. Lagging and sorry-assed, he limped away. In the distance, he heard Wallace singing to what looked like McGrady, who was down, but Horowitz's legs kept this game, walking. Through the woods meant Jeannie. Trains went to her, horses, wagons. A bullet brings a man away, why not to where someone was?

Horowitz only had one picture of his Jeannie, but it was top rail. The men had all sorts of perfectly lewd things to say about the hotdog she was holding, but Horowitz was a good sport. His sweetheart worked in an arsenal, building guns. Myles's girl looked a dream, but he got huffy if a soldier took too long looking. Fitsky's had very sensuous lips and right this minute was running a sock factory, so he claimed. The men pictured that home was swirling with girls, covered with it. In the bars, it was girls playing pool against girls. The beaches filled. In winter, sleds. Girls on skates. Snowball fights with girls.

Wallace didn't have a sweetheart. He was the only one. He tried to imagine himself jogging with Fitsky's sweetheart. Tossing socks to her in the factory. Cooking her all kinds of dinner. Wallace didn't even have a wife who had died or a sweetheart who was mad. He said the reason he didn't have a steady was he was an oversexed bachelor, that he had given more women 'the time' than he could count on both hands and feet. This was true. Wallace was nice-looking, confident, and came from a town of seven women to every man. In his town, they joked there was something feminine in the water. Recently, they'd found something in the well supply, but it wasn't hormones or shampoo, just an unhealthy amount of metals, giving teeth a blue tint. But Wallace loved to talk sweethearts, while McGrady grew quiet when talk turned that way, as it often did in the evenings, causing Wallace to believe McGrady was the most lovesick of all, and Myles to think it was humbug, there was no sweetheart to start with.

Lodi and Rogers knew each other from before. They hung close together, compulsively making jokes. Wallace knew army men took on new habits. Men found themselves singing and whistling away, using all sorts of slang, praying, counting. Lodi was constantly putting caterpillars on men's backs, wailing nonsense from pretended bad dreams. One time, Lodi made and wore a hat of flowers while Rogers laughed himself into a fit.

Beautiful, mutated, hungry for kisses, dripping slime. Wallace pictured McGrady's Sweetheart shaving hairy thighs, fiddling with the clasp on a Tiffany's bracelet. Loading up firearms, ruining a pie. So what if it was mutant as Lodi said, scaly skin, turkey neck. No one can tell a soldier who to love, only who to kill. With McGrady dying in his arms, he found such slogans easy to come up with. Trees are hard friends. Rocks don't know shit. War doesn't build character, it reveals it. That would look fine, sewn on some army banner in the Mess Hall, thought Wallace. Here was a brief moment in which Wallace felt he could compose any number of hit songs, haikus, or improvisational routines, but like moments, it ceased, crashing invisibly into the next.

Horowitz found railroad tracks and happily limped alongside. He'd shot, skinned, and ate a rabbit for breakfast. The railroad reminded him of a story of McGrady's.

Back where McGrady called home, a new railroad line was hammered down and one part went deep in some woods. Neighborhood kids would scour the tracks for dead animals. Animals hadn't yet gotten the hang of these trains, would occasionally freeze terrified when one came barreling by. Kids would bring these smashed possums home in a burlap bag, lay them out to marvel, tease the little sisters. One day McGrady goes and all alone and dead on the tracks is a squirrel, but wearing a tiny tuxedo. This part made the soldiers all laugh and Horowitz had to explain what a tuxedo looked like to Myles. Myles said, So, it was someone's pet then? McGrady said, No, just a fancy ass squirrel. This got the boys wheeling. Myles said, Was it a doll? Life-like, done good? McGrady snorted, No, figure this squirrel came across a perfect-fit suit in the woods, looked good, felt right, and went about his life like that, in style.

Myles didn't believe it. He went off at the mouth calling *liar*. Said McGrady's Sweetheart was a phantom made-up one, and the well-dressed squirrel another hallucination. Wallace whistled. Myles jabbed his bayonet in McGrady's direction, wrathy and fit to be tied. McGrady just turned and grinned. Oh boy, McGrady said to Myles, You're the kind who can't trust the clouds to stay up. Always fearing they might fall and wreck your house. McGrady stopped to stare at the bayonet's sharp tip, then continued. Now, I don't bluff Myles. But me and you are different kinds. You need to hold a piece of something to understand it. So, some luck ever understanding anything of mine. Myles let his bayonet down a little, his arm tired. McGrady went on, Go back to your tent and do whatever it is you do. Spare us your personality for a while, go on. Myles didn't budge, just sat there pouting. Van Creerie was taken with the story and often when they saw something strange or miraculous, he would say, Like a squirrel in a suit! And everyone would find themselves agreeing.

Alone with cold McGrady, no new blood, all dried, browned, Wallace missed the boys. The area around him was jokeless. His mind made nauseous connections and to keep calm, he strained to remember the sweetheart pictures. Every warm-blood in that troop would admit they'd spent too much time with those pictures. They got passed and passed around. Culler's picture wasn't even photographic. His was a drawing his sweetheart had done from the mirror. Lodi's was taken at a fair and there was a phony backdrop of mountains painted behind her. Wallace could still picture Horowitz's, standing in a summer dress, holding a hot dog, smiling to herself.

Jeannie looked at a picture of Horowitz and then set it down on her dresser. She closed her eyes and tried to remember Horowitz's laugh, but the laugh that rang in her head was of her old school boyfriend, George. George had the greatest laugh, completely surprised like he hadn't at all planned on laughing, hadn't known what laughing was, and here he was, doing it, laughing! When George laughed it seemed that there was nothing else important, and hurrah for that, because it sounded like he was not anymore capable for anything else. When George laughed it made Jeannie laugh, which made George laugh, which made Jeannie, made George, Jeannie, George; so naturally Jeannie sought to make him laugh, dancing around, trying out voices, asking strangers peculiar things, and their times together were sure lively. At the orchestra once, George with his hiccups, but he couldn't help it! Poor George! It was a recurring ailment of his, really. He would hold his throat with horror. But Horowitz! Who was more sincere than Horowitz? And smart? With a build that could carry Jeannie out from burning houses. Jeannie would set fire to a house just to have Horowitz carry her off! And Horowitz was the better kisser, had tons more tact. But if she were to remember who was the friendliest, the best at conversation with strangers, then it wasn't George or Horowitz, it was that terrible rat of a man she went with one summer, who only wore knickerbockers in loud tweeds and wished her to part her hair on the opposite side of what was usual for her. He did excel at putting people at ease, though a temporary, formulaic ease. But if she could take different qualities from different men and arrive with a new man, this new man could not beat Horowitz. The mixing wouldn't work. This new man would be some sociopath for sure, a problem man who lay on your breasts and couldn't ever push himself off, whispering, adorable misfit whose shyness gave him hives, or a loudmouth advertiser for useless horseshit. Oh Horowitz, Jeannie said aloud, wherever you are, come home and I'll make you a sandwich while you cry.

McGrady's Sweetheart lived in a swamp, had grown gills, wore a necklace of fish eyes, killed boar, raccoons, stole bird eggs, baby crocs, ran screaming from porcupines, shivered in the night. Rode around on an alligator, counting its scales. Scientists camped out to research the creature. They pressed sweaty binoculars to their faces. They wrote in their journals, "McGrady's Sweetheart demonstrates the variation possible in a species."

McGrady was cold and unresponsive. Wallace's legs were asleep, but he did not move. He knew it was time to dig a big hole and hug his losses, but he sat there bored and stunned. It was his fault. The wilderness breathed leaves, bugs, breezes. Nothing was anyone's fault. The wilderness alluded to change. The wilderness was inhuman. Wallace stroked his moustache nervously. The wilderness was a place, was a force, covered the earth, and *he* was just a thing inside it. Humans warm and with skin, houses of uneven wood planks, the ground the bottom, the sky real high. Wallace put his hand on McGrady's face. Eyes closed, mouth closed, but a nose stays the same. Open and closed. A nose is like a statue, thought Wallace. A nose is most like clay. A nose is the sculpture of a face, thought Jeannie, staring hard at the picture of Horowitz. A nose is for fun. A face wants to say something forever and forms the nose, stuck forward, to present the rest of the face, thought Jeannie. Wallace nodded. A nose is defiant. Stubborn and undisputed, thought Jeannie, touching her own. Wallace settled back against his tree. It was grainy dark in the woods around him, the moon awake and glaring.

Fitsky skedaddled after a short skirmish with the enemy. Lodi and Rogers soon after. Myles saw Lodi leave, but when he objected, Lodi ran over and punched Myles black out, then ducked into the woods, trigger finger poised, looking for a country road. Van Creerie didn't want to jump to conclusions. A lot can happen to a soldier, he said thoughtfully to Myles. It was down to Van Creerie, Myles, and Cullers. This sure wasn't the plan, said Van Creerie. One of them kept watch while the other two slept and like this they split the night in three. In daylight, they stretched their intuition and chose a direction. Their spirits swayed low, but then the sun would tease them between branches, or some deer would shyly glance their way. It was hard to resent the daytime, the weather just right. Plus, Myles didn't want to return to his sweetheart. He'd had his fill of her recently.

The picture Myles claimed and showed, was in fact, not his real sweetheart. His sweetheart was bossy and rail-thin Belle, who wavered between delirious sentimentality, and an aggressive idea of how things should be. Instead, he showed a picture of his cousin Wendy, whom he'd always found attractive. It wasn't rare for Wendy to have a lady bug walking the length of her finger. She was confident and strong like a very good song. He knew a girl like that was scarce as hens teeth. If he were to die in battle, he thought the ruined picture might be returned to his family, who would be sick with confusion, but somehow the gesture would make it to Wendy, and, well, she wouldn't be pleased either, but maybe at the funeral, she and he might have a secret, and a secret was alive, even when you weren't.

The scientists collected hair. Found a small hut of sticks and vines and staked out in the bushes for hours, nibbling on clover until they saw an old deadbeat returning home, beard to his waist. They questioned him about the creature, rolled their eyes when he feigned ignorance, then walked sullenly back to camp. They sat around the fire that night telling wizard stories, eating scraps. Then the talk turned to introduced species, all the wildtypes of mutated organisms: heterozygous, homozygous, compound, genetic, spontaneous, induced. They had a brief but emotional debate on extraterrestrial life, causing each to scamper off to their own tent and lay awake thinking.

The next morning, the woman scientist Meriweather collected bits of hair and feathers, bitten leaves. When she tried piecing together all she had gathered, pinning the feathers to the ground and sketching out some possibilities, she ended up with a nonsense animal, a made-up thing, a scarecrow, a costume, and was embarrassed. She walked to the swamp and collected a sample, but the flies were thick so she did not linger.

What about walks, thought Jeannie. My legs like them sure, but this hike wouldn't quit, thought Wallace. He looked at McGrady's dirt-covered boots. And what about wars? he thought, what's wrong with them? Too dramatic I think, thought Jeannie as she put down her picture. She crawled into her bed wearing all her clothing. With one foot, she pulled the sock off the other. Her cat John Singer Sargent hopped onto the bed in a single deft motion. What's good about cats? he thought, while she pet hers. She thought, To exist alongside, to be near them relaxed, calmly, sweetly, matter-of-fact. Wallace grinned and sat and waited. She petted John Singer and thought, What about bodies, houses, and grass? But she interrupted herself, How about families? She thought. He said, A good place to start. He ran his hand along the grass beside him, grabbed a few and pulled. He listened to the crickets chime and click their song. Now crickets, he asked, now what about them? She opened her window to listen. Natural collaborators in a close-knit community. He smiled and toyed with one of McGrady's shirt buttons, then realized and stopped. He had an eager feeling in his chest, like it was striving to get away. Like he might pass his hand over his ribs and hear a xylophone. He felt his breath in his nose and said quietly, Then what about love, tell me, how's that? Jeannie closed her eyes and ran a finger across her eyebrow. She said, Like having fun as a kid, feeling in common with the sky, a layer of varnish. Wallace found himself playing with McGrady's hair. Jeannie heard her sister knock on the door, but surprised herself by not moving a hair and holding her

breath. Her sister called her name and waited. Jeannie
waited. John Singer stretched a paw straight out in front
of him and licked his leg. Jeannie waited until her sister
padded down the hallway, then breathed out suddenly
and wriggled into her sheets. And God, she whispered
softly, how about him? Wallace looked around, moonlight
outlining the trees. His heart beat amateurly. The crickets
didn't quiet. The wind blew good and cold. God's not
here, he thought, but everything else sure is.

Cullers went in a baffling fashion. Dead in a way Van
Creerie and Myles didn't know. They'd been living an
experimental approach, making soap and foods from
whatever they found, and probably it was one of these
attempts at traditional living that did Cullers down, but
Van Creerie and Myles couldn't say. They spent a day
burying him, deliberating over what to do with the hand-
drawn sweetheart, eventually burying that too, though it
seemed a waste, a smaller additional loss.

Van Creerie had been nominated Sergeant because of
his great thick beard. He was billed as a community leader,
a fitness expert. Really, Van Creerie had little experience
besides cooking meat and coaching baseball. And he did
both beautifully at training camp. Barbequed up some
ribs and umpired a rec game. When making assignments,
they'd given Van Creerie only eight men, since he had
a dreamy manner unsuitable for war. His half-troop was

back-up for Sergeant Rangeley's men, many of whom had been injured and discharged.

Van Creerie couldn't find the heart to make his men follow the strict rules they'd learned back at camp. To march like wooden soldiers. He felt warmly for these boys who grew candid around the campfire. He had misplaced his order papers and maps. He hadn't known exactly where to direct his men, but figured he'd receive a sign. Maybe a telegraph man would approach them in the rain, dripping wet, mad as hell, telling them they were off their mark. Or a bird, with a message glued to his leg with gum. This outfit was supposed to be capable, so he'd submitted to his instincts, which led them into a very long camping trip. A retreat, he'd thought happily. Like had been forced on him in youth, in church.

Van Creerie and Myles were so far off track, it felt the only man they'd run into would be an old, ragged, rugged one, who did his living in the woods, and didn't even know there was a war on. They'd run into one such the week before and Van Creerie had started up a recruitment speech, force of habit, then trailed off distractedly. All their bullets were spent in a target competition Van Creerie had won with controversy. They began to finally feel their vulnerability. If the enemy were to approach them, all they had were two equally dull pocketknives. Myles had lost his bayonet heaving it after a fish. They began to dream other options. First matter at hand was to remove any identifying mark on their uniforms. It wasn't enough to rip off their badges. Van Creerie burnt parts of their clothes. Myles collected raspberries and made a dye.

Horowitz laughed for the first time since leaving his troop. He had just bought his train ticket when he saw the sign. *Stan Brady's Gentlemen and Ladies*. It advertised a traveling act. A crude painting of a man in hat and tails surrounded by animals dressed in formal wear. He wanted to tell McGrady. He found himself walking to the address of the theater. What a story for Jeannie! he thought. He spent a small amount on a ticket and aimlessly wandered the town before the show.

It was a small town, not unlike his own. He found a church, a library and a pond full of mallard ducks. Hungry, exhausted, miles and miles from Jeannie, he began to regret his latest decision, and then an earlier decision, and all the other ones that had come before. His life seemed hinged together in a faulty, inexperienced way, allowing whims and fate to beat it thin, and now it felt like a doomed thing he carried around with him. The ducks laughed. He picked up a rock wanting to nail a duck, but this pond was the center of town, these ducks weren't game. How had it gotten like this? Animals were now citizens, now performers too? The world was getting soft. He paced around the lake. The ducks laughed and laughed at him.

Stan Brady tried to calm his crew, but once one animal started squawking, the others couldn't resist. His raccoon, typically well-behaved, got aggressive towards the rooster, who was a new addition. The ostrich, which had cost him a fortune, spent the whole show trying to escape its dress, clawing at it with grotesquely large legs. The audience was a small but riled bunch that found the chaos hilarious, much better than the original plan of organized dance and ventriloquist song. This wasn't unusual. This work had its nights.

After a bad show, Stan would lock up the animals and venture out for a drink. Once or twice he'd returned with a devastated feeling, pacing the cages past midnight. The raccoon staring with its bright marble eyes. In Stan's hands, he'd held his rifle, but no animal knew that. Every time he'd ever thought of it, his raccoon would stare him down, and worst he ever did was free the misbehaving members of his crew. And who would call that *bad*. Animal is an animal and no nicer place to live than the world, sprawled and open, to live natural as an Indian. But who knew how training changed an animal. If somehow he had bred a desire to perform in these creatures.

This time, however, Stan's nerves were shot. The audience laughed at the wrong places. The dog crouched in an all too familiar way and Stan panicked. The rabbit was teething on a bit of oat stuck to Stan's sock and he bent down to brush it away. It was a liquid anger, a foaming, shifting, lava anger, a hot spread across his face, and in a wild, uncharacteristic move, he grabbed his rabbit by its bowtie and threw it into the crowd.

Asleep against McGrady, Wallace was awakened by a loud blast that sounded so close to his ear, every muscle in him gave a start. Then he fell down again, head back to McGrady, this time with blood, this time dumb, dead, and for good. The enemy soldier shook. He threw his gun down and cowered. He had never shot a man before. He crawled over to Wallace, then crawled away. He picked up his gun and slowly walked back to get a better look at McGrady's face. The enemy soldier admired McGrady's proportions, pleasant, inevitable. A twisted instinct in him urged him to stay with the dead and dying, but that was twisted, stupid, he grabbed his gun and got the hell out of there.

The enemy soldier walked with a swagger, wearing Wallace's helmet. In his head, he was boasting to his troop, who were setting up camp nearby. The already-dead soldier had looked pretty, like one of his sister's girlfriends. He had always enjoyed that friend. The soldier he shot had looked stupid sleeping. At first, he'd thought it was two dead soldiers, but then one had snored and with a knee-jerk reaction he yanked the trigger. His body had known what. He'd had trouble in his first battle, all the noise and men flashing by, but a sleeping man, he knew what to do with a sleeping man.

The creature waded into the swamp and crouched in the water, muddying its feathers. The swamp was still and the creature was still inside it. Flies flew in clouds. The sun blazed on like something broken. There was a splash as the creature dove and caught a fish. The creature brought the struggling fish to its mouth and scaled it with its teeth. With the collar of the fish stuck in the creature's mouth, the creature took a claw to the belly of the fish and tore upwards, towards the head. One claw forced through the bony portion between the fins. The other claw dug in and grabbed out the guts. With one claw of guts and the other with fish, the creature ate it all in a few bites, a crack each time a bone was chewed.

Pee On Water

Though alien to the world's ancient past, young blood runs similar circles. All those bones are born from four grandparents. Baby teeth and baby teeth all down the line. Jackets didn't used to zip up. There wasn't a single door.

Earth is round and open, whole and beating in its early years. The stars are in a bright smear against the blackboard. A breath pulled so gradual the breath forgets. Winds run back and forth. Clouds idly shift their shapes. Stubborn ice blocks will not be niced down by the fat sun. Melted tears run, then freeze. Tiny cells slide into tiny cells. The wind learns to whistle. The sun starts setting in a colorful display. Ice melts into oceans, lakes, and ponds. Plants have their first batch of leaves. Guppies shiver in the lake. Shiver, have babies, babies shiver. Crawlers.

Diggers. Stingers. The plants get bit and chewed. Leaves grow more intricate. Beings start dragging with them, little lives. Moments where they crawl on sand. Moments where they look behind them. They eat plants. They eat stomachs. Lick bones. They pee on grass. Pee on dirt. Pee on snow. Their skin is cut by teeth, by claws. Water fills their lungs. Blood cries itself in a blind pool. Blood dries on leaves. Blood browns on fur.

Creatures big as mountains stomp on top of mountains. Then new ones. New ones. Feathers, spikes, hooves. Clouds crawl smugly. The air smells cool. Atoms bump and lump. Birds have sex. Bears have sex. The sun gets better at setting. Monkeys play with sticks. Monkeys eat ants. They get sexy about each other's butts. The monkeys fuck from behind. They sleep in leaves, in mud, in trees. They protect their babies and teach them. The sun glares in their eyes, making spots.

Ants amble on, self-consciously changing direction. Rain makes them flinch, makes them happy. The monkeys make faces. The monkeys get smart. Two monkeys look at each other with knowing eyes. The trees sway. The birds chat. The knowing eyes are locked in a gaze. They look away. They look back. They have sophisticated children. The new monkeys need less and less protective hair. They have babies. They fight, throw punches, show teeth and bite. They think each other are sexy. Raise their babies away from the others. The new female monkeys have vaginas more between their legs, less likely to snag on branches. Males try sex with females from the front. Boobs get bigger to remind males what butts felt like.

This is the nice time of early men and monkeys, before cigarette butts cozied fat into the grass. No plastics, no prayers. Wood isn't sliced into slats, it's still living it up in trees. The rain is surprising, usual. Men and monkeys leave their lives with their bodies. Early men paint, cry, stare into fire meditatively. Pee on grass. Pee on dirt. Wear furs, have babies, catch dogs. Fall in love with dogs. Pause at oceans and their rambling edges. Sticks complicate grass. Grass complicates sand. The ground and every thousand thing on top of it. Curves and lumps. Uneven clouds. But click the clock radio through am to pm, spin the equal sphere like a sonic hedgehog. The leaves live the leaves fall, the leaves live the leaves die.

Men ride horses, roam plains, live in trees, in caves, wipe the sleep out of their eyes. They dance to a beat, carve wood into arrows. Pleasure and fun plus boredom and loss. The fun of hands gliding on top water. Of mud oozing between toes. Knotted hair is pulled back. Dirt gets comfortable on skin.

A band crouches in the bushes. Horses down, blood on ground. Blood on grass. Blood on brains. Legs are separated from bodies. Trees stand still, sway, stand still. The first restaurant opens. Families look alike. Caught dogs love man back. The middle of the night waits for people to run bravely through it. A toothbrush with bristles is invented. Dandelions lose petals, grow big fluffy heads.

Days of work. Hands on rakes. Hands on shovels.
Hands on rocks. Hands in clay. Hands in water. Aches
in bones, aches in muscles, aches in head. Night chases
day. Seasons switch slow. People pee in bushes, in open
trenches. There are jobs, schools, songs. There are Moms
and Dads. Young and carrying their children haphazard
down the street. Older and with their hands in dough.
Men feel cool riding horses. Arrows are pulled on tight
bows, yanked back near ears, released in wild flight.
Blood dries in sand. Blood dries in hair.

The sun casts pyramid shadows on packed sand. A
girl awakens to be seventeen. The heat is hot on the street.
Sand in teeth. "Sister!" her boyfriend says. He gives her
love poems written with the picture language. They are
about bathing together in the river, touching and holding
red fish. The girl laughs, "Brother, what fish?"

"The ones that feel right in hands." He nudges her.
He hunts honey all day. He and others sacrifice an
animal. Remove its lower entrails and fill the body with
loaves and honey and spices. They offer it to a god. The
boyfriend sneaks out to meet the seventeen-year-old
girl. They get drunk, tongue on tongue, tongue on lips,
tongue on cheeks. She puts honey and crocodile dung in
her vagina to block out sperm. They sniff water lilies, get
high, fall clumsily asleep.

Chairs are rare. They sit patiently in rooms. Mutton
fat is boiled to make soap. Rocks are fired out of bamboo

poles. Condoms are made from fish and animal intestines. Men feel cool playing the lute. They pee in private. Fish are caught with hooks. Held in rigid hands. Unhooked with fish eyes wide and watching, wishing for water, wishing for water. Diseases wriggle, latch onto cells, to genes, to skin. A bishop writes a book that recommends letting children have a childhood. He says babies should have their spirits stirred "by kisses and embraces," that "children should learn to play." Children say their jokes a few more times aloud. They balance their spoons on their noses. They lie in the flower field and hum.

A lake sits still and wet, creating dynamic calm. Girls no longer swim lakes. "Fish bite our thi-ighs!" A collective whine. The ducks don't give a fuck. "More for us." The ducks stick their face in their feathers. "You've chay-yanged!" They eye the girls, "You used to wear your hair in knots."

"Don't remind us." The girls watch the lake with the others, for the dynamic calm.

A rebellious inventor is sick of shit on the street. Of shit in bushes, of pee in puddles. He takes his evenings by himself, working hard on a necessary for his godmother, the Queen. His wife laughs. His friends laugh. He tinkers with pipes. Meanwhile, he shits in the outhouse. He smells pee on the sidewalk. He wants a machine that will whirl it all invisible. He succeeds in making a flush toilet. A plumbing wonder! He tries it out. Pees into the toilet. Each drop twinks. A pull of the flush and the toilet answers, a magic wave! The sewage system is not advanced enough to handle the water disposal. A smell creeps out the pipes. The inventor's friends laugh. He never builds another, though he and The Queen both use theirs.

The first chocolate factory. First personal ad. Friends add onto long running jokes. Young Beethoven goes deaf from his father beating the shit out of him. Dogs get annoyed at having their ears inspected. Deadly fever epidemics kill thousands. A band of adventurers plot to overtake something. The year without summer. June snow comes down in sheets. The seventeen-year-old girl gets arrested for wearing pants. First safety pin. First saxophone. A pencil with an eraser attached. Two people say the same thing at the same time and laugh. Diamonds are discovered in Africa. Diaries discovered in underwear drawers. First White House Easter egg roll. First train robbery. Boxers start wearing gloves. Flush toilets work with new sewage systems. Everyone begins to pee on water.

At the World's Fair, someone rolls a waffle and scoops ice cream in it. Plastic is invented. Neon lights. 127 kisses in a single movie. Fire department horses retire. Men feel cool riding cars. Chuck Berry fucks time into place, pulls it into beats and it hangs. It plays. Women use Lysol disinfectant in their vaginas to prevent pregnancy. Crowds of bodies are buried in the ground. Bombs are made with chemicals about to freak out. The seventeen-year-old girl looks into the toilet at the shape of shit that sits there, complete as one thing, a size similar to her boyfriend's penis. Not right, but close maybe, and she puts her hand above the water, widening her fingers to remember the length.

Cars come close to smashing. Flags paraded around, then stuck on the moon. A little sister orders her baseball collection by cuteness. Wild animals have no more room. Land gets so full of buildings, when town girls and city boys escape into the open, 'God' is waiting in the fields. Cars smash, glass in a crowd of shards. Huge ambivalent teen models lounge across highway billboards. Dust gathers between VCR remote buttons.

A bunch of 5th grade girls hang out with 5th grade boys and the boys start looking through the videotapes for something to show the girls. The girls don't know what but they giggle and try to sit up so their stomachs don't bunch but they bunch anyway. A boy sticks in the video and it's of a man raping a woman against a pinball machine. The 5th graders stare, leaving the potato chips alone in the bowl. A boy laughs. A girl tries it out, laughs a little too.

Dog walkers pick up after their dogs. Shit in plastic. Shit in trash. Shit on grass. Pee on grass. Pee on pavement. Pee on pee. Cars come close to smashing. Ketchup proudly won't leave bottle. Underwear inches up in butts. Bullets find their snug way into bodies. Moms and Dads talk in whispers while children pretend to sleep in the backseat. Snow falls all night, everyone wakes to good moods.

Guitars bought optimistically, lean grandly forgotten against bedroom walls. Raindrops race on car windows.

Harper dribbles the ball down the court, guarded by Ward, head fakes right, passes left to Pippen. Pippen up against Oakley, looks to see if Longley has posted, but Longley hasn't posted, Longley is tangled with Ewing. Longley's arms curl around Ewing while Longley's little eyes look to lock with Steve Javie's eyes, but Javie's eyes follow the ball. Pippen drives by Oakley, then passes to Kerr who bounces it to Jordan. Jordan holds the ball, his eyes twinkle. He passes it back. Alone behind the three-point line, Kerr takes a breath, grimaces, shoots the ball into a spiraling three-point attempt, which hits the rim and sails out of bounds.

Someone is killed wearing a Mickey Mouse shirt. Blood on head. Blood on mouse. Blood on pavement. The mouse still smiles. The sun is in a rhythm. The sky stays put. Babies grow into sturdier shapes. The rocks stay. The paintings stay. The people leave. Blood slows and then sits. Tongues get hot and hurt in their mouths. The sitcoms play on. Newly dead bodies get put in wood. Spacemen invade space. Dog catchers catch dogs. Then the sound, dirt on wood.

Girls sit outside a mall in the cold. One girl is sure life stops at dirt on wood. Black like outer space. But the seventeen-year-old girl says firmly, "When you die, you watch movie remakes of your life." The girls smile, but the cold tells them it is dirt on wood. A boy rides loops in the parking lot, his butt high off his bike seat. Sperm bite eggs. Wet new eyes. Tongues on tongues, dirt on wood.

Cell phones are used as weak flashlights. City teenagers discover grass. People strap bombs under their outfits and enter buildings. Religions are dragged through time. A pet dog catches a rabbit, hears his name called, turns around, loses the rabbit.

The buildings get straighter, sturdier, simpler, shinier. On New Year's, everyone looks funny in their 2020 glasses, 2050 glasses, 2086 glasses. Every famous person born finds the time to die. The newspaper isn't on paper. Scientists are still trying to make pain less painful.

Wake to half thoughts and a dirty mouth. Remember your first name and last. Toothpaste on the toothbrush. The day cut into hours. Stream your pee onto water. Remember the fields of trees, the wayward grass? We couldn't help crowd everything with squares. Dictionaries, mattresses, apartment complexes. All buildings with flat faces, with rows and rows of square eyes. Pages, screens, tiles. The curves got covered with lines. The birds have sex. The bears eat trash. Life still runs enough years. Plenty more than before. Fur ruffles in the wind. Candles coy and shy their hot face. Many parts are still the same. The day is light and easy to see in. A soap bar slims down to a sliver.

Rachel B. Glaser is also the author of the poetry collection, MOODS, published by Factory Hollow Press. She was the winner of McSweeney's 2013 Amanda Davis Highwire Fiction Award. Glaser studied painting at RISD and fiction at University of Massachusetts-Amherst. She paints basketball players among other subjects and teaches writing at Flying Object in Hadley, MA.

For more information visit Rachelbglaser.blogspot.com

Also from Publishing Genius

A Mountain City of Toad Splendor by Megan McShea

Night Moves by Stephanie Barber

Proving Nothing to Anyone by Matt Cook

Meat Heart by Melissa Broder

The Disinformation Phase by Chris Toll

We Are All Good If We Try Hard Enough by Mike Young

The Best of (What's Left of) Heaven by Mairéad Byrne

Words by Andy Devine & Michael Kimball

Easter Rabbit by Joseph Young

A Jello Horse by Matthew Simmons

Light Boxes by Shane Jones

*visit www.publishinggenius.com to order and see more books
also visit www.everyday-genius.com every day*

49594304R00088

Made in the USA
Charleston, SC
28 November 2015